MOVIN' DIFFERENT

A HOOD MILLIONAIRE ROMANCE

KEVINA HOPKINS

Mailing List

To stay up to date on new releases, plus get information on contests, sneak peeks, and more,

Go To The Website Below...

www.colehartsignature.com

PROLOGUE
MCKENZIE

This morning, I woke up on the verge of tears, and all I wanted to do was stay in bed all day. Something was wrong with me, but I didn't know what the hell it was. I could already tell it was going to be a long day based on the rocky start. In my rush to get ready for work, I didn't have time to properly comb my hair, and I ended up having to throw it in a ponytail and put on the first jogging suit and sneakers I saw. I hated going outside not looking up to par, but I hated being late even more. The last thing I wanted to do was give my supervisor a reason to bitch.

"Kenzie, when you finish your line, you can go on your lunch break," my friend Liam called out, pulling me away from my thoughts.

I was glad as hell to hear that because I had been on my feet for the past four hours, and I was hungry as hell since I hadn't eaten all day.

"Your change is $24.69," I said as I placed the money into the customer's hand.

"Thanks, shorty. Can I get your number with that?" he

asked and flashed a smile.

I inwardly rolled my eyes because I hated being called shorty. Like, even if I was interested, he had just blown it. Calling me shorty or a girl was the best way to be ignored.

"Nah, my boyfriend kills people," I replied seriously.

"Something tells me you're worth the risk." He smirked, still trying to shoot his shot.

"Man, she told your ass no. Now, move, so the rest of us can pay for our shit," the customer behind him yelled.

I work at Footlocker in North Riverside mall, so I was used to dudes trying to hit on me. I was only there to make my money and go home, though.

After another fifteen minutes, I was finally able to go to the food court and grab something to eat. I decided to order from **Steakhouse.**

"Can I get an Italian beef dipped well with nacho cheese and hot peppers? I want nacho cheese and mild sauce on my fries too with a Tropical Punch Mystic."

"Your total is $13.27. Will that be cash or debit?" the cashier asked.

"Debit," I replied before swiping my card.

I grabbed my condiments and utensils while I waited for my order. After a couple of minutes, I received my food then left to find a table. I found one close to the back of the food court, so I sat down and placed my headphones on, ready to enjoy my break.

I opened the food, and my mouth watered. The shit looked good as hell. You would have thought I hadn't eaten in days the way I dug into my food.

"Hmmm." A slight moan escaped my lips when I ate one of my cheese fries.

I had just broken a piece of my beef and stuck it into my mouth when I detected a presence in front of me. Thinking it was another thirsty nigga, I was ready to turn him down, but when I looked up, I noticed it was this bitch Shavon and her cousin Diane. I wondered what the hell Shavon wanted because she'd hated me ever since her pops and my mom got married.

"Uhm, can I help you?" I asked with irritation because all I wanted to do was enjoy my meal in peace, and these bitches were standing there like they were mute.

"I don't know if this is a good idea anymore," Diane called herself whispering to Shavon, but I could hear her ass clearly.

That piqued my interest because I wondered what they were plotting.

"Nah, fuck that. He doesn't have the right to treat you the way he does!" Shavon yelled.

"Would y'all tell me what the fuck is going on or get the hell away from my table," I demanded.

"You and that nigga not about to keep playing in my cousin's face. Let his ass know he got a baby on the way since he can't bring his ass home," Shavon spat.

I was so caught up in Shavon's words that I didn't realize she had taken something from Diane and threw it in my food.

When I looked down at my food, it was like the world stopped. All the music and noises faded into my background. I had blacked out, and it seemed like I was the only person in the mall. I couldn't believe this pit bull looking bitch had actually thrown a used pregnancy test in my food. Not even God himself would be able to stop the ass whopping this hoe was about to receive, and once I was done with her, he was going to feel my wrath.

I warned that nigga not to play with me when we decided to make it official. I told him I was a special kind of crazy, but I guess he thought I was playing, so now it was time for me to show him.

CHAPTER ONE
MCKENZIE

"Here we go again," I mumbled when I heard my mother's bedroom door slam.

That could only mean she and her husband were about to start arguing. I grabbed my Beats and put them on, then turned them up as loud as I could without them hurting my ears. I would be glad when my stepfather found a new job, then maybe his ass wouldn't be so grumpy. He hadn't worked in the past three months since he got laid off, so all he did was drink and find things to bitch about.

All I wanted to do was lie in bed and relax today. I had flown back from Miami last night after being gone for a month, and I enjoyed the relaxation because I was never able to rest while I was out there. My family always had some shit for me to do since they didn't see me often.

"Kenzieee," my sister sang my name as she burst into our bedroom.

I took my headphones off and looked at her because I knew she was up to something. "Yes, Aniyah?"

"Get up and get dressed, so we can go outside. Charmaine

just called and said there's a basketball tournament going on at Garfield Park today. Uncle Craig is about to drop her and Tori off over here now, so hurry up."

"Girl, I'm not trying to be sitting at that damn park. I'm tired. You know I just got back."

"Come on, please? You been gone a whole month. The summer is almost over, so you know we all not gon' be able to hang out as much. Liam is playing in the game," she said, referring to my guy best friend.

I did not want to go to that game, but at the same time, I didn't want to let my sister down. "Okay, but as soon as they start acting crazy, we're leaving, or I'm leaving y'all ass."

"Bet. I'm about to go tell Ma while you get ready," Aniyah said before leaving the room.

I climbed out of bed and searched through my drawer for something to wear. Although I wasn't in the mood to go, I still needed to look my best. There was no telling who I would run into while I was there. All the get money hood niggas made sure to be in attendance, and the thirsty hoes looking for a baller were waiting like bait.

I took a Burberry short set from my drawer and some fresh underwear, so I could take another shower. I had showered this morning already, but it was hot outside, and I didn't like putting on fresh clothes before I washed my ass.

After grabbing my robe and everything I needed for my shower, I left my room and went to the bathroom across the hall from my bedroom. I turned on the hot water then brushed my teeth while I waited for the water to get hot. Once I finished brushing my teeth, I climbed in. I couldn't have been in there longer than two minutes before someone started banging on the bathroom door.

"What?" I called out.

"Hurry up. I have to use the bathroom!" my brother Tyrese

yelled.

"No, I just got in here. Go outside and use it."

"Hell nah, hurry your ass up. I don't know why you ain't tell nobody you were about to go in there anyway," he yelled.

I scoffed at his response. Who in the hell would announce that they were going into the bathroom? I didn't even know he was home because he was usually on the block or with one of his girls around this time. Ignoring his response, I continued to shower for another ten minutes. He was lucky I had somewhere to be, or I would have been petty and stayed in there longer.

I climbed out of the shower and dried off, then put on my robe before going back to my room. I hated having to rush out of the bathroom for people. That was just another thing on my list of reasons why I couldn't wait to move out.

Don't get me wrong now, because I didn't live in the slums or a run-down apartment. I had never been abused or missed a meal a day in my life either. My mom made sure we had clean clothes and a hot meal before we went to bed every night. If I'm being honest, I was actually spoiled as hell. I was just over living in this house and my mom's husband.

Sometimes I felt like the walls were caving in on me, and I was going to suffocate. There were five of us living in a three-bedroom house with one bathroom. I was eighteen years old and sleeping on a twin-sized bed since I shared a room with my nineteen-year-old sister. I literally had no privacy unless she was out.

I couldn't complain to anyone, though, because it was my choice to continue living there. When I was fourteen, my father invited me to move to Miami with him and my brother Martez, but I declined because I didn't want to seem insensitive to my mother's feelings. I lied and said I didn't want to start over at a new school and that I'd miss my friends and family in Chicago.

The truth was, I didn't want my mom to think that what she did for me wasn't enough. She already had the notion in her mind that I loved my father's side of the family more than I loved hers. That wasn't the case, though. They just provided a different lifestyle for me.

My father owned a seven-bedroom, eight-bathroom house in Miami, and my bedroom there was bigger than two of the bedrooms in my mom's house plus the bathroom combined. Per my mother and father's agreement, I went down there every other holiday, spring break, and one full month during my summer break. My father and brother, in turn, came up here every other month for one week, so I could spend time with them. At first, it felt like a lot because I hated flying, but I'd come to love it.

It was only a matter of time before Aniyah would come in and start rushing me, so I hurriedly moisturized my body and then got dressed. Once I was dressed, I took my scarf off and combed out my wrap. Before I flew home yesterday, I had gone to the shop and got my hair dyed honey blonde with a blowout. I grabbed a ponytail holder and stuck it in my purse just in case something jumped off, and I had to pull my shit in a bun. There were a few bitches in the streets who hated me just because I was breathing.

I put on some Mac lip gloss and my Burberry sneakers to match my outfit. Afterward, I stepped back and admired myself in the mirror. My Burberry shorts stopped two inches past my ass, and the pushup bra I had on under my v neck shirt had the girls sitting pretty.

"Damn, I'm bad as hell," I said aloud as I admired myself in the mirror.

I was what people liked to call slim-thick. At 5'6, I was 140 pounds with curves in all the right places. I didn't have big breasts or a big ass like the girls you see on social media, but I did have enough up top for a mouthful and enough in the back for a handful. My beauty alone was enough to keep someone's attention.

"Kenz, come on. Tori and Charmaine are on the porch waiting," Aniyah announced as she barged into our bedroom.

"Okay, here I come. You can't rush perfection, you know," I replied.

Aniyah rolled her eyes at me and left the bedroom. I grabbed my purse and car keys then joined everyone on the porch.

"It's about time. I was about to come get you myself," Charmaine said.

"Girl, bye. Your ass would've just been sitting there, waiting for me to get ready," I said as I walked off the porch and to the driveway. I hit the alarm on my cocaine White Lexus IS that my dad bought me for my birthday, and we all piled in.

I connected my phone to the radio, and we sang off-key to Beyoncé during the fifteen-minute drive. Once I found a park, we all touched up our lip gloss and hair before getting out of the car. I locked up, then we walked through the crowded park, causing heads to turn because we were all bad as hell.

Tori wore a pair of black shorts and a white shirt with some white Forces on her small frame. She had her signature short red hair slicked to the back, showing off her high cheek bones on her light skin. Charmaine and Aniyah both chose to wear jersey dresses with high heels. They had their DD breasts and Big Booty Judy asses on display. Charmaine had a 20-inch Brazilian weave, and Aniyah had long box braids.

I scanned the park in search of my friend Liam. The park was so crowded that all I saw was a sea of people everywhere. The DJ had bitches twerking their asses and niggas bopping their heads to Juvenile's "Back That Ass Up." On the other side of the park, dudes were talking shit and shooting dice.

After searching for almost five minutes, I finally found Liam talking to some of his teammates. I went to speak to him while my girls went to talk to Aniyah's boyfriend and his friends.

"Hey, best friend," I spoke as I approached Liam.

"Hey, Kenz," he responded as he stood up to hug me.

"Can I be your best friend too?" a dark-skinned, handsome dude asked.

"Nah, I'm the only guy best friend she needs," Liam said.

"Look at you not wanting to share and shit," I teased.

"You already know you're my future wife," Liam half joked.

All I could do was smile at that because I didn't want to hurt his feelings. Liam was always like that when guys tried to talk to me while he was around. I had known Liam all my life. Our mothers grew up together, and they said it was destined for us to be together. In a perfect world, Liam would be the love of my life. We'd have kids and grow old together. Too bad my world wasn't perfect, though.

Any female would be lucky to be in a relationship with Liam. He was tall, dark, slender, and handsome as hell with a great personality to match, but he wasn't my type. Liam was too nice for me. I couldn't be with a guy who would allow me to push him around. I guess it's true what they say about females being into guys who were like their fathers because I loved me a bad boy. Hopefully, it was just a phase, and I would break out of it when I got older. For the time being, though, Liam and I were sticking to friendship. We lost our virginity to each other, and I let him give me head a couple times because he wanted to practice, but other than that, we'd been cool.

It was almost time for the game to start, so I excused myself and went to join my girls and the group of guys with them. I spoke to everyone, then went to stand by Charmaine.

"McKenzie, when you gon' be eighteen?" K.G. asked.

"Why?" I countered.

"Because I'm trying to take you out, but I ain't trying to catch a case in the process."

"I'm already eighteen. My birthday was last month," I replied, even though I would never go out with him for a number of reasons. He was a man whore who went after anyone with a vagina. The other reason was I had my eyes on his boss.

"Man, leave that damn girl alone. She doesn't want your ass," Tino said, causing his guys to laugh.

"Nah, she wants me. She just doesn't know yet." K.G. smirked.

Tuning the guys out, I turned my attention to the game. I actually enjoyed watching basketball, so I loved the tournaments, unlike my sister and cousins, who only came so they could be nosey and be up under the guys.

"That's what I'm talking about, Liam!" I yelled when he made a dunk.

I looked down at my phone and saw that I had a text message.

Chase: *You looking good as hell right now, ma. You gon' come to my crib, so I can give you your birthday gift?*

Me: *Yeah, just let me know when you're there.*

Chase: *Okay. I got something to handle first, but I should be there by 7.*

Me: *Cool, I'll see you then.*

"What the hell got you smiling so hard?" Charmaine whispered.

"Chase asked me to come over after the game to hang out."

"Okay, girl, don't do anything I wouldn't do." Charmaine laughed.

I laughed at my cousin because that meant I was free to do anything.

CHAPTER TWO
CHASE

I was chilling and trying to watch the game with my boys, but at the same time, I couldn't keep my eyes off McKenzie's pretty ass. She had a light caramel complexion with some of the clearest skin I had ever seen in my life, complemented by light brown, almond shaped eyes, and deep dimples. Her hair was naturally curly and stopped at the center of her back. She hated wearing it curly, but that was the way I loved it most.

I had known McKenzie for about a year. We met through my boy, Quan, since he fucked with her sister. Sometimes when Aniyah came over, she would bring McKenzie with her. While they would be in the backroom chilling, I would sit around to keep her company. We'd watch movies, play the game, or sometimes just talk. I tried to keep my distance because shorty was only seventeen at the time, and I was twenty. I couldn't help feeling like a pedophile because of my attraction.

Not only was I attracted to her beauty, but her personality drew me in as well. McKenzie was a cool, down to earth ass female to be around. She was stuck up, with a slight attitude problem, but it was nothing I couldn't handle. I didn't like my bitches friendly anyway, so I didn't have to worry about her entertaining other niggas when I wasn't around.

"You ready to rob the cradle, baby bro?" my big brother Tino asked low enough for only me to hear.

"Man, she's eighteen now, so I don't have to worry about going to jail. She's feeling me too, though. We texted almost every day while she was away. She just waiting on me to make the first move."

"Well, you know you got to take a different approach with her. She ain't like these other thirsty broads that be on your dick," Tino advised me.

"You know I'm always up for a challenge."

The game went on for about an hour and a half. Afterward, people stayed around to kick it, but me and my crew had business to take care of. We said our goodbyes and were on our way.

I pulled up to my trap and dapped it up with a few of my workers before going in and down to the basement. Looking at two of my young workers tied up in chairs, I couldn't help but shake my head. I gave these niggas a chance to break bread, and they wanted to steal from me.

I grabbed a metal chair and set it in front of them.

"Where the fuck is my money?" I barked.

"I don't know. I swear I didn't touch nothing. I gave them what I had!" Al cried.

"Shut the fuck up with all that crying and tell me where my shit is before both of you catch a bullet."

"Dre has your shit. I told him it wasn't a good look to keep none of it," Al confessed.

"What? Al, you a bitch," Dre barked.

"Damn, lil' nigga, you tricking and shit. It looks like you about to piss on yourself." I laughed.

"Real talk, Chase, I'm going to keep it real with you. My granny needed help with her medication and the rent. I promise I can work off what I stole," Dre said.

I sat back in my seat for a minute, thinking about my next move.

"Yo, K.G., untie Dre and give him your burner," I instructed.

K.G. did as I told him, and a look of relief swept across Dre's face, but he had to know he wasn't about to get away with stealing from me. He could've come to me or Tino, and we would've looked out for him.

"Thank you, Chase. I appreciate this, man," Dre said.

"Don't get too excited because this is what's about to happen. I don't fuck with snitches, and I can't have them in my camp, so you're about to help me get rid of one. Kill your boy before you go, and you have two weeks to make up for what you took, or you'll be put down next," I warned.

"Dre, please don't do this," Al begged.

"Do it before I take the deal off the table, and I kill both of you."

"I'm sorry, Al," Dre told his homey before he let off one bullet into his head.

"Now, get the fuck out!" I yelled.

Dre handed K.G. the burner then ran out of the room. I knew he was probably running outside to release his guts because that's what I did when I caught my first body at fifteen.

My brother Tino and I had been in the game for almost six years, and we got our money from the mud. We grew up in a two-bedroom row house in the Vill. Our mother worked as a home health care worker at the time while going to nursing school. The money she made was only enough to cover the bills and keep food on the table. Trying to take care of a thirteen and sixteen-year-old boy was expensive, so Tino and I decided to start making our own money.

It started off as nickel and diming in front of the crib. We loved the thrill, but the money we were making still wasn't enough because we wanted to get our family out of the hood. So, we hit my uncle up, and he fronted us on our first brick. That went on for almost a year until we had saved up enough to skip the middleman. Our uncle put us in contact with his connect, and we put our own crew together.

After that, we took off, and you couldn't tell us shit. We went from flipping bricks to doing hits. We were down for anything that involved putting money in our pockets. By the time I was fifteen and Tino was eighteen, we were able to buy our OG a house.

We bought a six-bed, four-bath duplex in Berwyn. Our mom had one of the houses, and Tino and I stayed in the other connected half until he moved out two years ago to live with his baby mama. I bought another crib last year for myself, but I still went to my old house when I wanted to hang out with my people or didn't feel like driving to Schaumburg.

I gave K.G. an order to get rid of the body, then I headed up the stairs to check on everything else.

"What you about to get into?" Quan asked.

"Why? What's up?"

"I'm trying to see if I can get the keys to the crib, so me and Niyah can chill for a minute."

"Nigga, you need to stop being cheap and move out of your OG's crib, so you can have your own place to fuck your bitch. She got to be tired of coming to my crib with you to do it."

"Nah, she straight. She knows I'm saving up to get a nice house for us," Quan said.

"You can't get the keys because I'm on my way there. Y'all can come through, though."

"Thanks. Good looking out," Quan replied.

I dapped him up then left so I wouldn't be late. It was 6:39 pm when I made it home. I rushed into the house to take a quick shower before Kenzie got there. By the time I was done showering and putting on some basketball shorts, she was texting to let me know she was outside.

I put on a pair of socks then went to open the door. Her sweet perfume hit my nostrils when she walked into my house. She had changed her clothes and was now wearing a short white sundress. I couldn't help pulling her into my arms and holding her tight. I had missed seeing her lil' ass in person over the past month.

"Let me find out you missed me." She smiled, showcasing her deep dimples.

"You know I missed you, ma. Are you hungry? I can order us something," I offered.

"No, I'm fine. Aniyah said something about she and Quan were going to grab something before coming over here."

"Okay, well, come to my room, so I can give you your gift."

"Uhm, what kind of gift do you have for me?" she asked as her eyes scanned me skeptically and stopped at the bulge in my shorts.

"Not that, baby girl. You not ready for him yet," I told her.

Kenzie let out a sigh of relief before following me into my bedroom. I reached into the closet and handed her the light blue Tiffany bag. She opened it and smiled hard as hell when she saw the heart necklace and bracelet set.

"Oh, my God! I love it, Chase. Thank you!" she beamed before jumping into my arms.

I smiled because that was the reaction I was looking for. I didn't know what to get her lil' spoiled ass.

"You're welcome, baby girl."

I caressed her cheek and leaned down to kiss her just as my doorbell went off.

"That's probably Quan and my sister," Kenzie said and took a step back.

I was ready to beat Quan up for ruining the mood.

"You're right. Why don't you find a movie, and I'll go let them in?" I suggested.

I walked out of the room and headed back to the front of the house. When I opened the door, it was Quan, K.G., Tino, and Aniyah. They had food, alcohol, and weed on hand.

"Where's my sister? I saw her car outside."

"She's in the room, looking for a movie for us to watch."

"Why y'all got to watch a movie in the room? Don't be in there trying to fuck on my lil sister," Aniyah said.

"Mind your business. I'm not going to do shit to her that she doesn't want. I ain't tried to force myself on her in all this time, and I'm not going to now."

"Here, bro, I'll roll up a new one," Tino said and passed me a blunt.

I took the blunt from him then grabbed a couple bottles of water before walking back to my bedroom. Kenzie was sprawled out across my bed with the intro of *Money Talks* coming on. I could get used to having her in my bed. I closed the door then climbed in with her.

I lit the blunt and closed my eyes while I hit it. After a couple more pulls, I handed the blunt to Kenzie. She dragged the blunt between her pouty lips, letting the smoke come out of her mouth. The sight had my dick jumping. We passed the blunt back and forth one more time before I put it out and pressed play on the movie. I could feel her stealing glances at me, which was proof that she was feeling the kid.

"You like what you see or something?" I asked. I wanted to see if she was going to try and flex on me.

"What if I do?" she challenged.

I gently grabbed the back of her neck and pulled her into a kiss. Her plump lips were as soft as I imagined they were. I could only imagine how they would feel on my manhood. Deepening the kiss, I slipped my tongue into her mouth, surprising both of us because I wasn't into sticking my tongue down a female's throat. I broke the kiss and made a trail from her jaw to her chin, then finally her neck. I sucked as gently as I could, but I knew I was going to leave my mark on her light skin.

Kenzie let out a light moan as I slid my fingers up her dress and into her underwear. I gently rubbed her clit, then slid two fingers inside. Her shit was tight and wet. She rotated her hips and rocked back and forth on my fingers as I picked up the pace. If I didn't know any better, I'd think she was still a virgin.

"Are you a virgin?" I asked.

"Nooooo," she moaned as she started to cum on my fingers.

I removed my fingers from her canal and licked them dry. I could tell she ate a lot of fruit because she had a sweet taste.

"Let me eat your pussy," I said.

She looked like she was debating on it before she finally spoke. "I don't know if this is a good idea."

"Shhhh, just lay back and let me handle my business."

I didn't have to tell her twice. She pulled her dress up and underwear down, then spread her legs wide, giving me a full view of her pretty pink pussy.

I kissed her inner thighs and blew on her clit before flicking it with my tongue. Then I tongue kissed her pearl as she arched her back and pulled my head further into her. She worked her hips, making sure we stayed on the same rhythm.

"Damn, Chase, I'm about to cum!" Kenzie cried as she tightened her grip on my head.

I continued to slurp on her pussy like a dog drinking water after being left outside in hundred-degree weather.

Kenzie tried to run, but I wasn't having it. I held onto her thighs and continued to devour her ass. I slipped one finger inside of her and then another. I tried to slide in a third, but it wouldn't fit. As bad as I wanted to put my dick in her, I wouldn't try because I could tell she wasn't ready yet.

"Wait, Chase, stop! It feels like I'm going to pee," she said, trying to stop me.

"Let it out for me, baby," I told her.

On command, her body jerked, and she squirted all over the place. Her pussy tasted so good; I was ready to dive back in, but I could tell she couldn't take any more right now. I climbed out of bed and went to the bathroom to brush my teeth and wash my face. I wet a wash towel with warm water and soap, so I could clean her up. When I walked back into the room, I chuckled. Kenzie looked like she could barely keep her eyes open. I cleaned her kitty for her then pulled her close to me.

We lay in comfortable silence before Kenzie spoke up.

"Why didn't you try to go any further?"

"I don't want to rush you into anything. I told you, you're not ready for this dick yet, but I'll give it to you in due time."

"You're just so confident that I'm going to let you hit, huh?"

"Yeah, I am. I'm pretty sure if I had tried to slide in you tonight, you would have let me," I told her honestly.

Kenzie got quiet after I said that because she knew it was true.

We chilled until about ten o'clock, then she left to go home. She had me horny, and my dick was hard as hell, so there was no way I would be able to fall asleep like that. I threw on my shirt and shoes, then drove to my girl Diane's crib.

I used the key she gave me to let myself in and walked into her bedroom. She looked like she was sleeping peacefully. I hated to wake her up, but I needed a nut.

I stripped out of all my clothes then climbed in bed behind her.

"Hey, baby. I didn't know you were coming over tonight," she said.

"Yeah, I missed you," I replied as I slid my hand under her shirt. I played with her nipples and in her love nest with my fingers until she was wet and ready before climbing on top and sliding deep inside of her.

Diane dug her fingers into my back as I went deep into her guts. We stayed in that position for a good twenty minutes before I busted on her stomach.

Diane climbed out of bed to clean herself, but I was too tired to move, so I just closed my eyes and went to sleep.

CHAPTER THREE
MCKENZIE

"Kenzie, are you alright?" Aniyah asked as she shook me awake.

"Yeah, why you ask that?"

"You were mumbling in your sleep, and you have tears in your eyes."

"I'm okay," I tried to assure her.

She looked at me skeptically before walking back out of the room.

I reached up and wiped the tears away. The dream I had felt so real. It had been a few months since I'd dreamed about Chris, my ex. I couldn't help but think it had something to do with me getting close to Chase over the past week. Even though Chris had passed away almost a year ago, I still felt like I was cheating on him if I entertained another guy.

Chris and I met when he was seventeen, and I was fifteen. He was my first love. You couldn't tell me that boy wasn't my future husband. I was head over heels in love with his bad-boy attitude, and I stayed fighting bitches to prove that I was his rightful girl. He claimed that he wasn't cheating, and I believed him because he gave me no indication that he was. I used to sit at the trap with him while he took care of his business. He was grooming me to be his ride or die. I was heartbroken when he got killed right in front of me. I could still see that shit sometimes when I closed my eyes.

Chris and I were on my block chilling like we did on any other typical summer night. Everyone was out playing music and kicking it.

"You know I love you, right?" Chris whispered in my ear before kissing my neck.

"I love you too, baby." I smiled back at him.

"No matter what happens, always remember the love I have for you."

Hearing Chris talk like that had me nervous. He always told me he loved me, but he never took it this far.

"Is something wrong, baby?" I nervously asked.

"Nah, everything is good. I just wanted you to know how much I love you. When you finish school, we gon' get a crib together, and you gon' have my babies."

"How many babies we talking?" I asked.

"We have to at least have two, so they don't grow up spoiled and lonely. I want a little boy with my swag and a little girl with your beauty."

"Okay. We can name the boy Christopher Jr. and our daughter Chase."

"Yeah, I like those names," he said as he gave me a cheeky grin.

"Then it's settled, but we'll have to move out of the city once they're born."

Christopher nodded his head in agreement. We sat and talked for another hour about our imaginary future.

"Bae, let me up for a minute. I'm about to run to the store to get us something to drink."

"Okay, I can go with you," I offered.

"Nah, just sit here. It's late, and I don't need your momz tripping on you for leaving the house."

I stood up, and Chris pulled me into a hug. I held him a little tighter than I usually did. For some reason, it felt like if I let him go, he would slip through my fingers.

"I don't want you to leave me. Why don't you come in, and I can make us some Kool-Aid?" I suggested.

Christopher lifted my chin, and I stared into his brown eyes. He smiled at me, and I couldn't help but return the smile. It was like my soul was tied to him. He was still as fine as he was the first time I met him in the store two years ago. He was 5'9, 160 pounds, with a taffy complexion and a low fade.

"I'm not going to leave you, baby. I'm only going to the store up the street. I'll be back in less than five minutes," he assured me before kissing me on the lips.

As I deepened the kiss, he grabbed a handful of my ass. I could feel his manhood pressing against me, and I just knew that would stop him from leaving, but it didn't.

"Go see if your momz is sleep. If she is, tell your sister I'll give her fifty dollars to let us have the room to ourselves for a lil' while. By the time you done, I'll be back, and you can take of this problem you just started." He smirked.

I turned around, and he smacked me on the ass before walking away.

I walked into the house, and my mom was in her room asleep. My brother's room was empty, so that meant he was still out. I went to my bedroom, where my sister was lying in bed, watching TV.

"Niyah, can you watch TV in the front for a little while?"

"Why? I'm comfortable in here," she said.

"Chris wants to come in for a little while. He said he'll give you fifty bucks."

"Okay, but y'all better not be loud. You know Ma don't sleep hard," she warned me before leaving the room.

I grabbed some clean linen and changed my sheets before walking back out of the house. As soon as my feet touched the porch, a deafening sound rang through the air that pierced my ears.

Bang bang bang.... was the sound from one gun, then a different sound came from another one. Rat-a-tat-tat-tatttt, followed by a boom. My block sounded like I was on an army base. Everyone was running for cover, and I was stuck in place until my sister pulled me down. She tried to pull me into the house, but I wouldn't budge. It felt like my heart had stopped beating until the gun sounds ended.

"They got Chris," I mumbled.

"What are you talking about, Kenzie?" she asked.

All I could do was repeat, 'they got him.' I didn't even have to see his body. It was like a piece of my soul left when I heard the first shot. Once the shots died down and sirens were heard, I snatched away from Aniyah and sprinted down my stairs. As soon as my feet touched the final step, I turned to the left, and my baby was lying on the ground, two houses away from mine.

I ran to him and pulled him into my arms. Blood seeped from his mouth, and the white t-shirt he wore was crimson red.

"You lied to me, Chris. You promised me that you wouldn't leave me. How could you do this to me?" I yelled as I pounded his chest.

"Young lady, you have to step away," a paramedic told me.

By that time, I was in a daze, and I had tuned her out. I told him he didn't need to go to the store, and he didn't listen to me. I was beyond hysterical to the point that they had to examine me and give me a sedative. While they were doing that, another paramedic put a white sheet over his body. Across the street by the alley, they were putting sheets over two other bodies.

That night, three people died, and five more were injured. It was by the grace of God that I wasn't shot since my dumb ass was on the porch the entire time.

I fell into a depression after that. I wasn't eating or sleeping without being medicated. It got so bad that my mother threatened not to allow me to attend the funeral if I didn't take care of myself. There was no way I wouldn't see my baby one last time, so I snapped out of it until the day of his funeral.

I was a mess when I got to the funeral. I sat with his family the entire time and tried to stay strong for them. There was a female sitting a few rows behind us, crying harder than his family and me combined. I was curious to know who she was because I had never seen her before. When it was time for remarks, she went up front and told the story of how in love she was with Christopher and how he was the father of her five-month-old son, Christopher Jr. My heart shattered all over again. I wanted to kick that nigga's casket for his betrayal. He had actually planned an entire life with me, and he was already living with another bitch.

When I looked over at Christopher's mother, she didn't seem surprised, so that told me this hag knew the entire time. I was at her house on the regular, and she was smiling in my face, knowing her son was living a double life. I got up to leave, and she tried to grab me, but I snatched away. I had to get far away from that funeral as fast as possible before I smacked her lopsided wig off her head.

There I was, seventeen years old, stressed and heartbroken over a nigga who was playing me. I gave him my all, only for him to be a liar and a cheater. He was good at what he did because he never gave me any indication that I had anything to worry about. I wondered what he would have done if I had gotten pregnant for real and had a son. Would he finally tell me he had a baby on me, or would he still let my dumb ass name our son after him? That was one thing I guess I'd never know since that nigga was six feet under.

After I left the funeral, I went home and changed clothes, then called my father. I told him I needed to come out there with him to clear my head. I stayed down there for three months before I came back to Chicago. When I came back, I was a different person. Christopher had stripped me of my innocence. I had a no-tolerance policy for fuck boys, and I refused to let another man get away with playing in my face without feeling my wrath. Christopher taught me a valuable lesson, though. These dudes' family and friends are not your friends. My new motto became *fuck your mama*. Her bald-headed ass was gon' lie for you anyway because, at the end of the day, she birthed your bitch ass.

I had been avoiding guys at all costs because I didn't want them to wake up my crazy side that I'd suppressed over the past year. Chase was slowly but surely wiggling his way into my life. With the way that man sucked the soul out of my pussy the other day, had he whipped his dick out, I would have ridden that motherfucker like it was a horse at the Kentucky Derby. He just didn't know what he was getting himself into, trying to fuck with me. I hoped he wouldn't let my innocent face fool him because I could be a real bitch at times.

"Me and Tyrese about to go to my dad's house for a barbecue for my granny. Do you want to come?" Aniyah asked.

"No, thank you. I'm going to catch up on some reading and relax since I start work tomorrow."

My father and brother still gave me money, but now that I was eighteen, it was time for me to work and show that I could be independent. They agreed to me getting my own place when I turned nineteen. They would cover the rent for a year, and I would be responsible for paying the utilities and all my other bills. I planned to start school in the fall, so I could start my own business and wait for my rich husband to come along and take care of me.

After Chris died, I was homeschooled in Miami. My father thought it was best that I remain homeschooled when I went back to Chicago because I kept getting in fights. I missed out on prom and graduation, but I didn't care about any of that because I didn't like half my classmates anyway.

Me having a job helped ease my father's mind some because he'd been worried that he was spoiling me too much, and I wouldn't know how to survive if something happened to him or my brother. I mean, I understood because, with the lifestyle they lived, they could be gone in the blink of an eye.

When I was thirteen, I went to Miami to visit my family for the first time, and that's when I learned my father was the head of his own empire. He has his hand dipped in everything from casinos to arms dealing and weapon trafficking. He wanted to shield me from what he did, but at the same time, he knew he had no choice but to tell me because I needed to be prepared if anything ever happened.

I climbed out of bed and grabbed my robe and caddy, which had everything I needed for my morning routine. Then, I walked into the bathroom and turned on the hot water in the shower. After I released my bladder, I brushed my teeth before climbing in the shower. I stood under the water and allowed it to run over my body. Since I was at home alone, I could stay in the shower for as long as I wanted. I stayed there for about twenty-five minutes before I climbed out, dried off, then wrapped a towel around me and went to my room.

I moisturized my body and brushed my hair into a bun. Since I didn't plan to leave the house, I put on a pair of black leggings and a red tank top with a pair of socks. I hadn't eaten anything yet, so I went into the kitchen and made a sausage, egg, and cheese breakfast sandwich. After that, I grabbed my plate and an apple juice, then went back to my bedroom. Finally, I climbed in my bed and turned *Grey's Anatomy* on.

When I picked up my phone and saw that Chase had called me while I was making my food, a huge smile spread across my face.

I still didn't know what it was about Chase that had me feeling like I was ready to move on with him. I mean, he was fine as hell, standing at 5'10, 190 pounds with a bronze complexion and dark brown eyes. It was more than that, though, because he wasn't the first fine man with money who had tried to get with me. Usually, I took their number and texted here and there when I was bored, but I had never chilled with them the way I did with Chase. And I damn shole didn't allow them to touch me. I guess time will tell as I allow our situation to progress.

CHAPTER FOUR
ANIYAH

"Man, get y'all cheating ass out of here!" Tyrese yelled at Quan and me.

"It's not our fault that y'all losing." I laughed.

Quan and I were playing spades against Charmaine and Tyrese. They were losing as usual, so Tyrese wanted to claim we were cheating.

"Why didn't Kenzie come with y'all?" Charmaine asked.

"She said she was tired and wanted to relax," I replied.

"Aww, I hope she's alright," Charmaine stated with concern.

"Girl, she good. She was out with Chase last night and got in late."

"Why is this my first time hearing this? How long her and Chase been talking?" Tyrese jumped in our conversation.

"Honestly, I'm not sure. I know they been cool, but they been spending time alone this week without me around."

"Why didn't you stop her? You see what she went through with Chris. She's too young to be in a relationship with a man like Chase," Tyrese pointed out.

"You know I can't stop Kenzie from doing anything, and I damn sure can't tell her who she can and can't date when I'm dating someone in the same profession."

Tyrese was about to reply until my aunt Cathy walked over.

"Hey, y'all. Where's McKenzie?" Aunt Cathy asked.

"She's at home. She wasn't feeling well when I left," I lied.

I didn't want my family to think my sister was acting funny and didn't want to be around them all of a sudden.

"I hope she feels better. Make sure you get her a plate to go when you leave."

"Okay, I will, Auntie."

"Mama wants to take a picture with you three," Aunt Cathy said.

Tyrese, Charmaine, and I got up and walked over to where my grams was sitting with my father and uncle Craig.

"Well, if it isn't my triplets. Come give Granny a hug." My grandmother smiled.

If it's not obvious by now, although Tyrese, Kenzie, and I were close in age, we had different fathers. Well, Kenzie did. Tyrese and I had the same father. My family called us triplets because Charmaine could actually pass for our sister more than Kenzie. We all had the same oval eyes, almond skin, and plump lips. I guess it made sense because Charmaine's father, Craig, and my father were twins.

The way my aunt Cathy told us the story, my mother and father were high school sweethearts. They were together until I was six months, then they broke up due to them growing apart. A few months later, my mom and her friends went down to Miami for a girl's trip and were on some baldhead hoe shit. She met a fine man by the name of Victor. He was mixed with black and Dominican.

Since my mom had just gotten out of a relationship, she wasn't looking for anything serious. My father was the only man she had ever been with, so she felt like it wouldn't hurt to have a little fun for once. It wasn't like she was going to see Victor again once her trip was over.

My mom exchanged numbers with him, and he offered to show her and her girls a good time while they were on vacation. The way he was splurging and buying bottles, she knew he had money. Not only did he have money, but he was also a smooth talker because he talked her right out of her underwear the first night they hung out.

Victor and his people kicked it with the ladies for the five days they were there. My mom enjoyed her time and went back home as planned. Victor was a distant memory until two months later, when my mom started having morning sickness. She went to the doctor and found out she was indeed pregnant. Although she knew it was Victor's, she didn't say anything until after Kenzie was born. She wanted to allow him to get a DNA test right off top.

When my mother called, she thought Victor would act stupid or try to deny my sister, but he wasn't like that. He hopped on the first flight he could get to Chicago that same day and took a DNA test. Then he waited in town until the results came back. Once the paternity was confirmed, he signed the birth certificate, and they came up with how much money he would give her each month.

My mom didn't know Victor from a can of paint, so she didn't trust sending her child to another state. Consequently, the only time he got to see my sister was when he flew into town. That's when Kenzie's father and brother started coming to visit her for one week every other month. It stayed like that until Kenzie was thirteen years old. After that, she was able to start going down to Miami with him. At that point, Victor started giving Kenzie money of her own and buying her expensive gifts.

Kenzie didn't act funny or stingy with me. She was always giving me something, even though my father gave me an allowance. Tyrese had his own money since he called himself being a dope boy. I say called himself because all his money went on clothes, shoes, bitches, and his damn car. One would have thought he would have been trying to get his own place to entertain them since he was twenty-one, but I guess that would be too much like right.

If everything goes as planned, I should be moving within the next year. Quan was saving up to get us a house. I had been looking for a job, but my father didn't want me to work since I would be starting school soon. I was going to take dental assistant classes and work at his office.

We stayed at my grandmother's house until almost ten, then we headed back to my house.

"Do you want to come in?" I asked Quan.

"Yeah," he replied before climbing out of the car.

Quan and I walked into the house, and my mother's bedroom door was closed, so we beelined to my room. When we entered, Kenzie was asleep with the covers over her head. I put my finger up to my lips to signal Quan to be quiet. He sat on my bed while I gathered my things to take a shower.

I walked into the bathroom, released my bladder, and took a quick ten-minute shower. After I moisturized my body and put on a baggy t-shirt, I entered my bedroom and found Quan lying under the covers. I put my things down and climbed in with him. Since it was a twin-sized bed, we had to lay on our side.

Quan wasted no time sliding his hand under my gown and playing with my kitty. A slight moan escaped my lips. The shit felt good, and I was close to cumming when he stopped. He reached over and grabbed a condom from my nightstand, then put it on and slid inside me. I pushed my ass back against him, so he could get a good rhythm. Quan was kind of on the chunky side with a six-inch fat dick. His stroke game was a bit weak, so there were only certain positions we could do in order for me to cum, and this wasn't one because his shit kept slipping out. Usually, I would have to be on top or have him hitting it from the back.

This went on for another two minutes before I was like, *fuck it*. I stood up from the bed and bent over, so he could hit it from the back. I just prayed that Kenzie stayed asleep and didn't catch me with my ass in the air.

Quan slapped me on the ass then rammed his dick inside of me. He held onto my waist while I attempted to throw my ass back on him in hopes that he could find my spot.

"Shit, baby," I'm about to bust," Quan grunted.

Nigga what?

"Okay, baby, cum for me," I whispered.

Quan only had two more pumps in him, and then he came in the condom.

"Damn, your pussy good as hell, ma. That's why you're going to be my wife one day," he said.

To say I was pissed would be an understatement because I needed a good nut.

I got up, pulled my shirt back down, and tossed the condom in the trash next to the bed.

"I need to sneak you back out before my mom comes out of the room."

"Okay, baby. I know you didn't cum, but I gotcha tomorrow. We're going to Chase's crib, so we'll have more time and room."

"Alright, I can't wait," I stated with fake enthusiasm.

I walked into the hall first, and when I saw that my mom's door was still closed, I rushed Quan out of the house. After giving him a quick kiss, I walked back to my room, grabbed my vibrator, and went to the bathroom to finish what he couldn't. All it took was three minutes before my body started shaking, and I squirted everywhere.

I cleaned myself and the toy before going back to the room. When I entered, Kenzie was sitting up in bed.

"Quan left already?" she asked.

"Yeah. I needed to get him out before Mom woke up."

"That was fast. I don't know how you do it. You're too young to be having whack sex. I'd been done cheated on him by now."

"It's not that simple, Kenzie. I love him, and I can't just break up with him because the sex is whack."

"Says who?" she countered.

"You wouldn't understand, Kenz."

"I'm just being practical, Niyah. I get that you love him, but if you continue letting that nigga think you enjoy the sex, he's not going to change. Stop faking and teach him how to eat it and beat it. I know you tired of replacing those damn batteries."

I couldn't believe I was getting schooled about sex by my little sister. That was one thing about Kenzie, though. She was going to speak her mind, and we had always been open with each other about everything. She had more experience than me, and from what she told me, Chris took care of his business. And if she was fucking with Chase, then I knew she was getting her back broke because I had heard stories about him in the past.

Quan was the only person I'd ever had sex with, so I didn't know what good sex felt like. I guess it didn't bother me because I wasn't missing anything I had before.

"Are you and Chase fucking?" I asked, changing the subject.

"Nah, we just be hanging out. He gave me head, but we

haven't had intercourse yet. I do plan to take a ride on that pony soon, though. My period was cockblocking, so I couldn't do anything, but that bitch left yesterday, and I'm ready like Freddy." She laughed.

"Just be careful and try not to get your feelings too caught up with him."

"I know. I'm not in love with him or no shit like that. He got me curious, and I'm sexually attracted to him, so I'm going to let him hit, and then we'll see what happens after that." She shrugged.

I shook my head then got in my bed. Sometimes I wished I could be as carefree as my sister. I didn't lose my virginity to Quan until I knew that I loved him.

CHAPTER FIVE
CHASE

I finished up my runs, then went home and took a shower, so I could get ready to meet up with everybody at the circle. I had a towel wrapped around my waist and was brushing my hair when a set of arms wrapped around me.

"Babe, am I moving in here with you when my lease is up, or are we renewing it again? We've been together for almost three years, and we could save a lot of money. We love each other, so I don't get what we're waiting for."

I sighed and turned around to look at Diane. Grabbing her arms, I pulled her on the bed with me.

"Baby, I'm just not sure if I'm ready for that yet. With the lifestyle I'm living, you already know I'm barely at home, and I don't want you up at night, waiting for me."

"What difference does it make if I sit here on my own or at my apartment on my own? This house is big, so if you need space to take care of business, you have that big ass basement and your mom's house. Unless you need a place to fuck other girls at."

"Come on, ma, it's not even like that. You can move in."

"Thank you, baby. I can't wait for us to live together!" Diane exclaimed before kissing me.

"You're welcome, ma. I need to finish getting ready, so I can head out to my meeting," I lied.

Kenzie had agreed to spend the night with me tonight, and I wasn't about to miss out on that.

"Okay. I'm about to go home, so I can clean up and do some laundry."

Diane had been at my house for the past three days, so I had been coming home every night at a decent hour. I hadn't been able to spend as much time with Kenzie as I wanted since she had started working. I lied to Diane this morning and told her I had some business to handle tonight, and I was going to stay at my old house.

"Alright, text me when you make it home."

"Okay. I love you," she said.

"I love you too," I replied before kissing her.

I really did love Diane; I just wasn't in love with her like she was with me. We had known each other since we were kids. Her mother was strung out on drugs, and her father wasn't stable enough to raise her, so her aunt got custody. They used to live next door to us in one of the other row houses, and her aunt and my mother were best friends. Although we moved, my mom stayed in touch with the aunt, and they came to our house all the time.

It wasn't until Diane was eighteen that we crossed the line. Her father had passed away from heart failure, and I had been there, trying to keep her from falling into depression. I decided to take her out to dinner, and afterward, we went back to my crib to chill. We were drinking, then one thing led to another, and I ended up taking her virginity. Then she told me that she loved me and wanted us to be together.

I loved Diane like a friend, but after taking her virginity, I felt like shit. Since I didn't want her to think I was taking advantage of her, I agreed on us being together. I figured I could grow to love her the same way she loved me since I was attracted to her. She was beautiful, 5'7, thick, with a toffee complexion. Her body wasn't perfect, but I didn't care about that. I loved her big titties, big ass, and pudgy stomach.

A year after we got together, Diane told me she was pregnant. I didn't want my child to grow up in the city, so I moved her into her own apartment out in Schaumburg and helped by paying half of everything for her. When she was three months pregnant, she had a miscarriage, and right after that, her aunt was diagnosed with breast cancer. I didn't want to leave her out there by herself because she was depressed, so I bought this house to be close. When I purchased it, she thought that meant she could move out of her apartment and in with me, but I told her it was too soon.

Being out in these streets, I encountered my fair share of temptation. I cheated from time to time, but it was mostly getting some head or a quick fuck. It wasn't like I was selling bitches hopes and dreams of us being together. I got what I wanted from them, then sent them about their way. I never strayed far and always found my way back to Diane. Her position had always been secure in my life. Well, at least that was how it was until I met McKenzie. I didn't know what it was about her, but she made me go the extra mile. I didn't want a quick nut from her—I wanted all of her. Her young ass had me eating her pussy and spending money. She and Diane were the only two females who could ever say I put my mouth on them.

McKenzie was the complete opposite of Diane in every aspect of looks and personality. They were both beautiful but different sizes and complexions. Diane was quiet and clingy, while Kenzie was a firecracker who didn't mind being alone.

Ironically, Kenzie and I had more in common than Diane and I did for her to be so young.

I got dressed in a pair of black Gucci jeans, a black and white Gucci shirt, and a pair of black Gucci sneakers. After putting on a few squirts of my Creed cologne, I slipped on my diamond cross chain, earrings, and diamond Patek watch. Finally, I grabbed my wallet and keys then headed out of the house.

I hopped in my black Lexus truck and took the twenty-five-minute drive back to the city. I stopped at the liquor store to grab a bottle of Patrón and two packs of Backwoods before driving to the circle. Once I got there, I drove around until I found my people. I parked next to McKenzie's car and climbed out.

The circle was packed as usual. There were motorcycle and car clubs out. People were playing loud music from their cars, and half-naked women were putting on a show. Bottles and blunts were passed around within groups. I hung out there on a regular, but I didn't like Kenzie being out there because the night always ended in a shoot-out. I'd rather be at the house chilling with my crew instead.

I spoke to everyone then looked for McKenzie. I scowled when I saw her talking to some nigga on a motorcycle. Whatever he was saying had her cheesing and showing her pearly white teeth. I waited patiently for almost five minutes until she came over to where we were.

"Hey, Chase," Kenzie spoke.

"Hey, McKenzie. Who was that you were talking to?"

"Just somebody who lives by my house." She shrugged.

"Aww, so y'all talking?"

"Damn, you in the wrong person's business right now," she said and rolled her eyes.

"Stop fucking playing with me before your eyes get stuck in

the back of your head," I warned.

"Nigga, y'all together now or something?" Quan asked me.

"Don't worry about all that. Her lil' ass know what time it is," I replied.

"Whatever. You doing the most right now, and all I let you do was taste the pussy," she mumbled so only I could hear her.

I gently grabbed McKenzie by her arm and pulled her toward my truck. I lifted the back and sat down, pulling her on my lap.

"Why you trying to play me like I'm some kind of lame?"

"Ain't nobody trying to play you. I was just being real. I'm not your girl, so you don't have the right to know who I'm talking to. I don't question what you do when we're not together."

"You could if you wanted to, though."

"Maybe, but that's not my place."

All I could do was nod my head because everything she said was true. Neither of us belonged to the other, so we didn't have the right to question each other, but I wasn't ready to let up yet.

"What if I wanted to change that? I'm trying to make you my girl." The words slipped out of my mouth like butter.

"You're not ready for a relationship with me, Chase. I might be young, but I'm a different kind of breed. My ex was a drug dealer before he got killed in front of me, so I know how this shit goes. You're surrounded by nothing but bitches who want to jump on your dick, and it don't matter how much I do it for you, you're going to let them do it."

"You can't cut off all men just because of what your ex did to you. I'm not gon' lie. I got bitches, but I'm willing to cut them off for you," I said, telling half the truth. I was willing to cut off everybody except Diane for Kenzie because, like she said, she was a different breed.

"We don't have to get in a relationship just because you want to fuck. We both know I was going to let you hit anyway." She smirked.

"That's not what this is about. I like you. I've been liking you for a while. I just wanted to wait until the right time."

"Okay, I'll give us a try, but I'm letting you know right now. Don't try to play me because I promise you will see a different side of me when I find out," she warned.

I swallowed the lump in my throat after hearing those words. Diane and Kenzie didn't run in the same circles. Diane never came out to the city unless she was visiting her aunt or cousin. Kenzie didn't know about my house in Schaumburg, so I was good as long as I didn't fuck with any other girls.

"You don't have to worry about that. Now, give me a kiss," I demanded. I grabbed Kenzie by the back of her neck and kissed her sloppily.

"Get down!" I heard someone yell.

Everyone started to scramble as bullets flew through the air. I grabbed Kenzie by her waist and shielded her with my body. I wasn't sure where the bullets were coming from, but I wanted to protect her either way.

Once it was silent, I sat up and pulled Kenzie out of the truck.

"Are you alright?" I asked as I examined her body.

"Yeah. Where's my sister and cousin?" Kenzie countered.

"Get in your car. I'll go see if I see them."

I waited for Kenzie to get in her car, then I walked down a few cars where I saw my crew getting up from their crouching positions. Tori, Charmaine, and Aniyah were standing there as well.

"Where's Kenzie?" Aniyah asked.

"She's in her car. We're about to get up out of here. I don't feel like dodging any more bullets tonight."

"Okay. Dell having a party tonight. We can all go there," K.G. suggested.

"Nah, I'm good, but y'all can go. I'm about to pick up some food and chill with Kenzie at the crib."

"Cool. We can all chip in and grab a few pizzas, then go back to your crib and hang out," K.G. said, not getting the hint.

"Man, didn't you hear what he just said? He not trying to hang with our asses tonight. He got all the company he needs waiting for him," Tino said. My brother always knew what the vibe was without me having to spell it out.

"Oh, damn, my bad. I didn't know y'all was close like that," K.G. stated.

"Yeah, that's my lil baby," I admitted with a smile.

I said goodbye to everyone then stepped to the side to talk to Tino in private.

"Can you drop Charmaine and Tori off at home if they not going to the party with y'all?"

"Yeah. I might come stay at the house tonight if I drink enough, but I got my key, so you don't have to worry about me disturbing y'all."

"Alright, good looking out." I dapped Tino up and turned to walk away when Quan's ass approached me. I already knew what this nigga was about to ask.

"Can me and Niyah come to your crib tonight since Kenzie is going to be there anyway?"

"Y'all get one hour, and that's it. Kenzie's a big girl. She doesn't need y'all there every time she chills with me," I pointed out.

"Alright, one hour is cool," Quan said.

I shook my head, then told Kenzie to follow me. I called in an order to Taco Bros, then drove off. By the time we made it to the restaurant, our order was ready. After that, we left to go to my house.

CHAPTER SIX
MCKENZIE

When we made it back to Chase's house, Aniyah and Quan were right behind us. I was kind of disappointed because I thought we would finally have the house to ourselves. Chase must've sensed my disappointment because he pulled me close to him.

"We're going to chill and watch a movie. By the time it's over, they'll be gone, and we'll have the place to ourselves."

"It's fine. You don't have to kick them out on my account."

"Nah, I already told him before we got here that he only gets one hour. I've waited all week to spend time with you alone, so I'm not about to mess that up for them," he told me.

I smiled, then we sat back and ate our food while we watched *Mr. and Mrs. Smith*. Chase didn't care too much for the movie, but I loved it. The concept had my attention from beginning to end.

When the movie had about twenty minutes left, Chase got up from the couch and walked to the backroom.

"It's time for y'all to get ready and go. Make sure to change those sheets because Tino is supposed to sleep here tonight," I heard Chase say.

Chase came back and started to clean up while I watched the rest of the movie. By the time it was over, Quan and Aniyah were coming in the front.

"I'm about to go, Kenzie. What time are you coming home?" Aniyah asked.

"I don't know, sometime tomorrow. I already asked Tori to cover for me. I called and told her I won't be home tonight."

"Oh, okay, well, I'll see you later then," Aniyah replied.

"See you."

Quan finished talking to Chase about something, then he left.

"Come on," Chase said as he picked up the bottle of Patrón and the blunts he had rolled.

I followed him to his bedroom and sat on the bed. He turned the TV on and sat next to me. Once he lit the blunt, we passed it back and forth while we took shots of Patrón.

The Patrón and Dro had me feeling good and horny. It helped ease my nerves some because I was nervous as hell to be there all alone with Chase. Making plans to have sex with someone and actually doing it were totally different. I grabbed my overnight bag and went into the bathroom to take a shower. I turned on the water, then released my bladder and brushed my teeth.

I tested that the water was at a comfortable temperature before climbing in. As I allowed the water to trickle down my body, I closed my eyes and got lost in the steam. After taking a fifteen-minute shower, I dried off and moisturized my body. I wrapped a towel around me then walked out.

When I entered Chase's room, the lights were dimmed, and he had turned the TV off. Slow jams played from the sound system. I looked at Chase and smiled before walking over to him. He pulled my towel from my body then pulled me on top of him. My lips crashed onto his, and he rubbed his fingers through my hair. Then he broke away and placed kisses on my collarbone and my neck.

I pushed Chase back on the bed and trailed kisses down his body. After I helped him out of his boxers, I slowly took the tip into my mouth and felt his precum slide down my throat. Inch by inch, I took him deeper until I felt his penis hit the back of my throat.

I sucked while twirling my tongue all over it.

"Fuck, Kenz, just like that," Chase moaned as he grabbed a handful of my hair.

I bobbed my head faster as he thrusted in and out of my mouth. After sucking a little longer, I moved my mouth from his dick and started sucking on his balls while jacking him. I could feel his balls tightening, so I knew he would cum soon.

"You like that shit, huh?" I purred before placing his dick back in my mouth.

"Slow down, baby. I'm about to bust," he announced.

"Come on then," I told him as I continued to handle my business.

"Grrrrrr," Chase grunted before releasing his cum into my mouth.

Chase flipped me over and wasted no time diving headfirst into my lady pond. He twirled his tongue around my pussy with no mercy. He was eating my shit like he had a point to prove.

I gripped the back of his head and held on to it while I worked my hips like a dancer.

"Right there, Chase. Don't stop, baby," I cried out as my toes curled.

He slid two of his fingers inside me. He wasn't as gentle as he was the first time he gave me head. That was probably his way of preparing me to take his dick.

"Cum for me, ma. Let me taste that sweet juice of yours," Chase demanded. He removed his fingers and smacked my pussy until I started squirting like a faucet that had just broken.

Me cumming didn't stop Chase from going back for seconds. I felt his tongue slither into my pussy hole and damn near jumped from the sensitivity. I tried to run, but he wasn't having it. He used his upper body weight to hold me in place as he continued to eat me like a starved animal. He didn't stop until I came all over his handsome face again.

Chase reached over to his nightstand and grabbed a magnum packet. He opened it and put it on before positioning himself at my entrance. Then he teased me a little before sliding the tip in. A moan instantly escaped my mouth and his as he opened my walls and pushed himself further in. I gripped his shoulder once he was buried all the way in me.

"Fuck, Kenz, you sure you not a virgin?" Chase groaned as he slowly thrusted in and out of me.

"Yeah, I'm sure. I've only been with one person, and it's been a year since I had sex," I confessed as my eyes started to roll.

Chase's mouth latched onto my nipple, and he bit it while picking up the pace, causing me to instantly cum on his dick. The shit Chase was doing had me feeling good as hell. I twirled my hips, making sure to meet him thrust for thrust.

"Cum for me again, baby," he whispered in my ear as he went deeper.

"Faster, Chase," I cried out as I gripped the sheets.

He obliged and picked up the pace, causing us both to cum.

"God damn, Kenz, that pussy like gold, ma," Chase said before lying back on the bed.

"I know." I pulled his condom off and tossed it in the trash can by his bed.

"Any niggas you been dealing with, dead that shit now. If I see you with anybody, I'm fucking both of y'all asses up," Chase threatened.

"What?" I asked just to make sure I heard him right.

"You heard me, McKenzie. You my girl now, so I'm the only one who should have your attention."

"You don't have to worry about that, Chase. You the only one that's had it in a long time," I admitted.

Chase pulled me on top of him and kissed me deeply. We rolled around the bed until I pinned him down, then reached over to his nightstand and grabbed another condom. I opened it and put it on him before gently sliding down his 9-inch thick dick. I rode his dick slowly until I was adjusted to it, then I rode him like I was at the rodeo. He held onto my waist and bounced me up and down. Grabbing my throat, he squeezed it gently, and I came all over him.

Chase flipped me over on the edge of the bed and rammed his dick into me. He grabbed my hair and pulled it as he murdered my pussy.

"Yeah, ma, give me all that pussy," Chase grunted.

The shit felt good as hell! I was on the verge of tears.

"Who this pussy belong to?" Chase demanded as he slapped me on my ass and fucked me harder.

"It's yours, Chase! Got damn, it's all yours, baby!" I cried.

"Good. Now cum on this dick," he ordered.

I threw my ass back, meeting his hard thrusts until he came in the condom. We both fell back, trying to catch our breath.

Chase pulled the condom off and tossed it before pulling me close to him. As soon as my head touched his chest, I passed out.

The following morning, I woke up to use the bathroom. Gently lifting Chase's arm, I slipped out of bed, careful not to wake him. I grabbed one of his t-shirts and put it on before going to the bathroom. After I released my bladder, I brushed my teeth. Since I was already up, I decided to see what he had in his refrigerator, so I could cook us some breakfast. He didn't have much in there, so I was only able to make pancakes, eggs, and bacon.

By the time I was done cooking, Chase had come in the kitchen wearing nothing but his boxers. I couldn't help but stare at his toned muscles, then my eyes trailed down to his morning wood. Flashbacks of last night came to mind, and my pussy started thumping.

Chase smirked before walking over and pulling me into his arms. He kissed me, and I could taste the toothpaste on his mouth. Then he spun me around, bent me over the kitchen counter, pulled his boxers down, and rammed his dick into me.

"Oh, shit, Chase," I moaned as he dug deep in my guts. It amazed me how easily he could find my spot.

I bit my bottom lip and twerked my ass as I came on his dick.

"I'm about to nut," Chase groaned as he pulled out and nutted on my ass.

"Our food is cold now." I laughed.

"It's going to be even colder because we need to shower," Chase said.

"You just trying to fuck in the shower."

"You damn right. We can warm the food up afterward."

After our heated shower session, we both got dressed and went into the kitchen. I stopped in my tracks when I saw Tino sitting at the kitchen table, eating the food I had cooked. My cheeks turned red with embarrassment; I forgot he was coming over last night. I wanted the floor to swallow me whole because Chase and I were both loud last night and this morning.

"Good morning," I awkwardly spoke.

"Good morning, Kenzie. Thanks for breakfast," he said.

"You're welcome."

"What the fuck you mean he's welcome? You didn't cook that for him. Now, what are we supposed to eat?" Chase asked.

"Relax, you can eat my plate. I need to be getting ready to go anyway, so I'll grab something at home."

"Alright, let me walk you to your car," Chase offered.

I went into his room, put on my shoes, then grabbed my bag.

"See you later, Tino. I hope we didn't keep you up last night," I said.

"Nah, sis, you good. I knew you was spending the night, so I slept with my headphones on." He shrugged.

Chase walked me to my car and gave me a kiss goodbye, then I headed home. By the time I made it home, it was 9:30 AM. I parked my car and got out. As soon as I walked into the house, I was face to face with my mother.

"Where the hell have you been, McKenzie?"

"I told you I was spending the night over Tori's house."

"Don't lie to me. I see the marks on your neck, so unless you and Tori got something going on, that's not where you were."

"It's not like that, Ma. I went to Tori's house afterward."

"I'm not trying to hear that shit, McKenzie. I was eighteen and hot in the ass before. I'm not raising no more babies, and we don't have room for none here," she warned me.

"Ma, ain't nobody about to have no baby," I tried to assure her.

"Okay, who is this boy anyway, and how old is he?"

I considered lying about Chase's age, but I figured what the hell. It was only a three-year difference right now. She didn't need to know he'd be twenty-two this year.

"His name is Chase, and he's twenty-one years old."

"Where do you know him from?"

"Oh my God, Ma. What's with the interrogation?"

"You just made eighteen, and you're living under my roof, so I have the right to know what you're doing and who you're doing it with."

"He's a friend of Quan's." I sighed.

"So, you're telling me that you haven't learned your lesson after what you went through with Chris yet? All you're going to do is end up heartbroken and alone again," my mother fussed.

"Well, it's a good thing I don't love him." I shrugged and walked away before she could say anything else. I was over the conversation, and I wasn't about to allow her to ruin my mood.

I walked into my bedroom and saw that it was empty, which I was grateful for because I didn't want the third degree from Aniyah. I couldn't understand why she had an issue with me fucking with Chase when she was fucking with Quan. Quan wasn't in the game as deep as Chase was, but the nigga sold drugs for a living too.

I shook the thoughts from my head and stripped out of my clothes before climbing in bed. Then I sent Chase a text, letting him know I was home before I closed my eyes and got a couple more hours of sleep since I didn't get much the night before.

CHAPTER SEVEN
CHASE

I climbed into the shower and closed my eyes, allowing the water to massage my body. This past year of my life had been hectic. Niggas robbing my trap houses, workers coming up short, and trying to maintain a relationship with two women. I've had to make my presence known more in the streets and buckle down on my team.

Ever since I moved Diane into my house, shit had been different with our relationship. She always had some shit to nag about, and she no longer cooked and cleaned like she used to before she moved in. It felt like the only thing going right in my life was McKenzie. She was like coming up for fresh air after holding your breath under water.

It felt like Kenzie was put on earth for me. She was so caring and understanding. I could have a long day at the trap, and she'd meet up with me just to chill and see if I ate. If I hadn't, she'd cook for me, and we'd sit back and talk about our day. I kept my word and got rid of all my other bitches. I didn't have the time or energy to entertain them while trying to balance Kenzie and Diane.

I still went home most nights unless McKenzie found a way to spend the night with me. I actually hated when I had to leave her and go home to Diane. McKenzie had just turned nineteen and planned to move into her own place soon. Once that happened, I knew it would be hard for me to juggle them both. Honestly, Kenzie was the only one I wanted to be with. It was crazy how my feelings had grown stronger for her than they ever were with Diane.

I regretted allowing Diane to move in with me because as bad as I wanted to break things off with her, I didn't want to leave her homeless. I had actually been thinking about whether I wanted to just tell her she could have this house, and I would move back to my old one until I could convince McKenzie to get one with me.

After finishing my shower, I walked into my bedroom, where Diane was lying in bed wearing a little t-shirt and thong. My dick bricked up just from looking at her. I felt like I was about to cheat on McKenzie, even though I was with Diane first. I was stressed and in need of a nut. McKenzie's cycle was starting, so she'd been cramping, which meant I wouldn't be able to get my dick wet with her today. It had been almost a week since the last time Diane and I had sex anyway, so I was like, fuck it.

I climbed into bed with Diane and spread her legs using my knees. Then, I lifted her shirt over her head and kissed her on the lips. She held onto the back of my neck and kissed me back. I broke the kiss and trailed kisses down her body. Finally, I ripped her thong and placed two fingers inside her.

She rocked her hips slightly as I picked up the pace. When I put my head between her legs and dipped my tongue in, she stopped me.

"Stop, Chase, you know I don't like that. I'm wet now, so just put it in," Diane whined.

I chuckled inwardly because Diane hated receiving and giving oral, while McKenzie, on the other hand, loved having my head buried between her thighs and slobbing on my knob. Releasing a sigh, I removed my hands and hovered over her. I slid inside her and lifted one of her legs in the crook of my arm, so I could get a good rhythm. Diane's pussy felt good as hell.

"Damn, D, your shit wet as hell, ma. Let me find out you missed this dick," I groaned as I picked up the pace.

"Yes, Chase, I missed it. I'm about to cum, baby," she announced.

I kept the same pace until she was shaking and cumming on my dick. Then I flipped her over and shoved my dick in from the back, pushing myself as deep as I could go.

"Ouch, Chase! Pull out some, baby. You're in too deep," Diane complained.

I groaned and pulled out some. She had just pissed me off by fucking up my rhythm. I was tempted to just pull out and go beat off in the shower because I was no longer in the mood. Closing my eyes, I pictured McKenzie throwing her ass back on me, and just like that, I nutted in Diane five minutes later.

Rolling over on my back, I threw my arm over my eyes as I thought about my dilemma. Diane had some good pussy, but it was a waste because our sex life was boring. She only liked to have sex in missionary or doggy style, and she couldn't take dick. She also thought oral sex was nasty, so I gave up on trying to convince her that it wasn't. I knew I was her first, so I tried to be patient and teach her, but it had been two years. If she hadn't learned to please me properly by now, I didn't think she ever would.

McKenzie, on the other hand, was the total opposite. I felt like I was going backward every time I slid up in Diane. Having sex with her was like a chore. Like I was doing it just because I was supposed to. When I was with McKenzie, though, I just wanted to live in her pussy. She allowed me to fuck her when-ever, wherever, and however I wanted with no complaints. If I looked like I was stressed, she'd slob on my dick without me even having to ask.

"I'm going to the city to see my aunt later, then I'm stop-ping to see your mom," Diane said, breaking me from my thoughts.

"Okay, I'm going by my momz after I finish taking care of my business."

"Alright. Can you just lay here with me for a little while? We don't get to do that often."

I pulled Diane into my arms and laid with her for about twenty minutes until she nodded off. Careful not to wake her, I climbed out of bed, grabbed a pair of boxers and my clothes, then walked into the bathroom to freshen up and get dressed. I had a slight headache, so I looked in the medicine cabinet to find some Tylenol when I saw Diane's birth control pills on the shelf.

I don't know what made me do it, but I decided to open them. When I saw that the pack was still full, I was instantly pissed. I searched through the cabinet to see if there was another pack somewhere, but I didn't see any.

I walked out of the bathroom and shook Diane awake.

"Diane, what the hell is this?" I yelled.

"Huh, it's my birth control pills," she said as she rubbed her eyes.

"No shit. Why the fuck is the pack full?"

"Well, it's been a couple years since I lost our baby. I thought now was a good time for us to have another one," she stated while fidgeting with her fingers.

"That's not a decision for you to make on your own. We agreed that the next time you got pregnant, we'd plan it together, and right now isn't a good time."

"I don't see what the big deal is. We live here together, and the right time will never come. It's not like we can't afford it, and you're not planning to leave the game anytime soon. I'm bored and tired of being at home alone. At least if I have a baby, I'll have something to do and someone to keep me company."

I looked at Diane's ass like she was crazy. I felt like she was trying to trap me and ruin my life. If I was to get her pregnant, there was no way I could break things off with her while she was pregnant, and I didn't want to raise a child in a broken home. I grew up without a father, so I always said that if I had kids, I would never put them or their mother through what I went through growing up.

My mother and father were in a relationship for about four years. She had Tino, and everything was good with them, but when she got pregnant with me, he was gone with the wind before her second appointment. Leaving her to struggle with a two-and-a-half-year-old while pregnant. He never attempted to reach out or pay child support. As far as I knew, his ass could be dead.

"I'm sorry, Diane. I can't do this anymore." I sighed as I sat on the edge of the bed.

"You can't do what? I know you not breaking up with me because I stopped taking the pill. We don't have to have a baby now. I can start back taking the pill."

"It's not just that, Diane. Everything is moving too fast for me. I wasn't ready for us to move together, and I'm not ready for a baby. We're not on the same page right now. We want different things."

"Really, so after everything I put up with from you, you're blaming me and calling it quits?" she asked on the verge of tears.

"I'm not blaming you, D. I'm not faulting you for wanting

more than what I'm ready to give. You're a good woman, and you deserve everything you want."

"I love you, Chase. There's no other person I want to be with. I can be patient with you. I'll do whatever you want. I know I'm not satisfying you in bed. You want me to suck your dick? I can do that. You want me to get freakier when we have sex? I can do that too. I'm willing to practice more. Please, just don't leave me," Diane begged as she burst into tears.

"This isn't about love, Diane. You know I'll always love you. We were friends before anything. I just need some time and space to myself to get my thoughts together. I'm going to stay at my old house for a few days, so you can really think about what I said, then we'll sit down and talk," I said as I pulled her close to me. I couldn't bring myself to break her heart even more and tell her that I was ending things because I fell in love with someone else.

I stayed with Diane for about an hour until she calmed down, then I grabbed some things that I would need at my old house before leaving.

I went to the trap and picked up Tino, then we hit the streets to do some drop-offs and pick-ups. After that, we chopped it up at the trap and counted money for a couple hours.

"What's up with you, bro? You look like you got a lot on your mind," Tino said.

"Yeah, I broke things off with Diane temporarily so I could focus on my relationship with McKenzie."

"I don't blame you. You should have ended things with Diane a long time ago. I look at the way you are with McKenzie, and I can tell she makes you happy. You gave it a try for the sake of y'all friendship, and now it's time for you to be happy before your luck runs out, and Kenzie finds out about Diane."

"You're right. That's why I ended things. I hate lying to

Kenzie, and being with Diane just seems wrong. I'm doing her more harm than good by stringing her along all this time."

I told Tino everything that had been going on in me and Diane's relationship, all the way to her trying to get pregnant without telling me. It felt good talking to my brother and getting everything off my chest.

I stayed at the trap for another forty-five minutes before leaving. On the way to McKenzie's house, I stopped at Walgreens and Panera to get a few things for her. After I parked, I sent her a text before grabbing the bags and getting out of the car.

Me: *Open your front door*

"Hey, what are you doing here? I look a mess," McKenzie said as she stepped to the side.

"You look beautiful," I replied, looking her up and down. She had on a pair of shorts with a baggy t-shirt, and her curly hair was pulled up in a ponytail on top of her head.

I followed McKenzie to her bedroom and sat on the bed with her.

"What do you have in the bag?" she asked.

"You told me that you were cramping, so I brought you some soup, crackers, chocolate, ginger ale, chips, and a heating pad."

"Aww, thank you, baby." She smiled.

"You're welcome. Eat your food, and I'll find us something to watch."

I flipped through her Netflix and turned on *Grey's Anatomy*. I hated the damn show, but it was one of McKenzie's favorites, and tonight was about catering to her needs.

Once McKenzie finished eating, she laid down, and I held her while she groaned in pain. I massaged her stomach, hoping to help ease some of her discomfort. I hated that she wasn't feeling good, and I couldn't take the pain away.

Whatever I was doing must have felt good because McKenzie fell asleep before the episode was over. I didn't want to wake her, so I just held her until I nodded off too.

"Kenzie, I'm about to go to the store. Do—" Aniyah stated as she burst through the room door.

I opened my eyes and looked up at Niyah, then down at a sleeping Kenzie. She was usually a light sleeper, so I guess that meant she hadn't been sleeping well lately.

"What's up, Niyah," I spoke.

"Hey, Chase, I didn't know you were here. I was coming to see if Kenzie wanted something from the store."

"Nah, she's good. I went to the store for her before I came over."

"Okay, I'll just sleep out in the front tonight," Aniyah said.

"You don't have to do that. We're only sleeping, Niyah." Kenzie groaned before turning to face me.

"Alright, I'll be back in a little while then," Niyah said before walking away.

I laid back down and kissed Kenzie's forehead. Since her bed was so small, we were up under each other like sardines. If she wasn't feeling bad, I would have suggested we go back to my house, so we both could be comfortable.

I lay there for about twenty minutes, just watching her sleep. I pushed a strand of hair from her face, and her eyes fluttered open.

I jumped slightly when she saw me watching her.

"Why are you being so creepy?" she giggled.

"Because I'm in love with you," I confessed.

Tears fell from Kenzie's eyes after hearing those words. "I'm in love with you too, Chase."

I leaned down and placed a gentle kiss on Kenzie's lips. If she wasn't on her period, I would have stripped her out of her clothes and made love to her in this little ass bed. This wasn't the first time I told her I loved her. The first time was three months ago, after we had just come back from a date.

"When you get off your period, I'm going to eat your pussy so good that you're going to pass out."

"I'm going to ride your dick so good you gon' be ready to wife a bitch," she countered.

Little did she know, I was ready to wife her young ass now.

CHAPTER EIGHT
MCKENZIE

The past year of my relationship with Chase had been pure bliss. I was hesitant in the beginning because I thought he would be on bullshit after we had sex, but that wasn't the case. He'd been caring, attentive, and cautious of my feelings. Even when I was a bitch and tried to push him away, he didn't budge. Eventually, I broke down and told him about my past relationship with Chris, and Chase assured me that I would never have to worry about that with him. He was possessive and jealous at times, but it wasn't the peeking through windows with binoculars kind.

I still had my moments when I wasn't sure if I could trust him because I knew how niggas in the streets were. I had popped up on his blocks and at his house, but I never caught him in a compromising position. He didn't have women calling his phone all day and night, and he made sure I was secure in our relationship.

After Chase told me that he was in love with me a couple weeks ago, our connection grew even stronger. Our sex had always been amazing, but now it was like he made love to my mind, body, and soul. He even suggested we move in together. As much as I loved him, I told him that was something I needed to think about.

Martez was actually coming out here in a couple weeks to help me find my own place. Him and my father didn't approve of me being with Chase at first, but eventually, they came around when they saw how good he was to me and how much I cared about him. I knew us moving together would be pushing it, though. I wasn't sure if I was even ready to take that step yet because I'd be damned if a nigga got pissed off and tried to kick me out. My father and brother would never approve anyway.

Martez is seven years older than me, and you can't tell him that he's not my second father. Whenever my father wasn't available, my brother was there for me. He was my confidant and the one person I could count on to be there whether I'm wrong or right. He'll hop on a plane the same day if I need him. My mother calls him about me more than she does my father.

This morning when I woke up, I was on the verge of tears, and all I wanted to do was stay in bed all day. I didn't know what was going on with me because I had the same feeling last night after I left Chase's house. I hadn't experienced this feeling since the day Chris got killed, so I didn't know why I was having it now. My first thought was that something was going to happen to Chase, but I quickly shook the thought away as just jitters from growing attached to him because there was no way my luck could be this bad.

Whatever it was, I needed to snap the hell out of it because I hated feeling this way. I could already tell it was going to be a long day based on the rocky start. In my rush to get ready for work, I didn't have time to properly comb my hair, and I ended up having to throw it in a ponytail and put on the first jogging suit and sneakers I saw. I hated going outside not looking up to par, but I hated being late even more. The last thing I wanted to do was give my supervisor a reason to bitch.

"Kenzie, when you finish your line, you can go on your lunch break," my friend Liam called out, pulling me away from my thoughts.

I was glad as hell to hear that because I had been on my feet for the past four hours, and I was hungry as hell since I hadn't eaten all day.

"Your change is $24.69," I said as I placed the money in the customer's hand.

"Thanks, shorty. Can I get your number with that?" he asked and flashed a smile.

I inwardly rolled my eyes because I hated being called shorty. Like, even if I was interested, he had just blown it. Calling me shorty or a girl was the best way to be ignored.

"Nah, my boyfriend kills people," I replied seriously.

"Something tells me you're worth the risk." He smirked, still trying to shoot his shot.

"Man, she told your ass no. Now, move, so the rest of us can pay for our shit," the customer behind him yelled.

I work at Footlocker in North Riverside mall, so I was used to dudes trying to hit on me. I was only there to make my money and go home, though.

After another fifteen minutes, I was finally able to go to the food court and grab something to eat. I decided to order from **Steakhouse.**

"Can I get an Italian beef dipped well with nacho cheese and hot peppers? I want nacho cheese and mild sauce on my fries too with a Tropical Punch Mystic."

"Your total is $13.27. Will that be cash or debit?" the cashier asked.

"Debit," I replied before swiping my card.

I grabbed my condiments and utensils while I waited for

my order. After a couple of minutes, I received my food then left to find a table. I found one close to the back of the food court, so I sat down and placed my headphones on, ready to enjoy my break.

I opened the food, and my mouth watered. The shit looked good as hell. You would have thought I hadn't eaten in days the way I dug into my food.

"Hmmm." A slight moan escaped my lips when I ate one of my cheese fries.

I had just broken a piece of my beef and stuck it into my mouth when I detected a presence in front of me. Thinking it was another thirsty nigga, I was ready to turn him down, but when I looked up, I noticed it was this bitch Shavon and her cousin Diane. I wondered what the hell Shavon wanted because she'd hated me ever since her pops and my mom got married.

"Uhm, can I help you?" I asked with irritation because all I wanted to do was enjoy my meal in peace, and these bitches were standing there like they were mute.

"I don't know if this is a good idea anymore," Diane called herself whispering to Shavon, but I could hear her ass clearly.

That piqued my interest because I wondered what they were plotting.

"Nah, fuck that. He doesn't have the right to treat you the way he does!" Shavon yelled.

"Would y'all tell me what the fuck is going on or get the hell away from my table," I demanded.

"You and that nigga not about to keep playing in my cousin's face. Let his ass know he got a baby on the way since he can't bring his ass home," Shavon spat.

I was so caught up in Shavon's words that I didn't realize she had taken something from Diane and threw it in my food.

When I looked down at my food, it was like the world

stopped. All the music and noises faded into my background. I had blacked out, and it seemed like I was the only person in the mall. I couldn't believe this pit bull looking bitch had actually thrown a used pregnancy test in my food. Not even God himself would be able to stop the ass whopping this hoe was about to receive, and once I was done with her, he was going to feel my wrath.

I warned that nigga not to play with me when we decided to make it official. I told him I was a special kind of crazy, but I guess he thought I was playing, so now it was time for me to show him.

It felt like an eternity before I snapped out of my daze, but it was only a matter of seconds before I jumped up, damn near knocking the table over to get to Shavon. I swung with all my might, causing her to fall to the floor.

"You-stupid-bitch! I-told-you-to-leave-me-alone!" I yelled as I punched her with each word.

Everyone stood around us, recording and egging me on while I got on top of Shavon and continued to punch her ass in the face. I wanted her to feel the pain she had just caused me. I wanted her to feel the pain I felt when she tried to fuck Chris while we were together. I wanted her to feel all the pain for the misery she had tried to cause me over the years. I had given her pass after pass, but this shit, I couldn't let slide. I wasn't even fighting her because she told me Chase was cheating. She was getting that ass beat because I was starving, and she ruined my lunch.

I banged her head on the floor until a pair of arms wrapped around my waist and pulled me up. That didn't stop me from repeatedly kicking her in her side, though.

"Yo, ma, chill. You gon' kill shorty," the stranger whispered in my ear.

I ignored him and stared at Diane, daring her to try me, but all she did was hold her head low and try to check on her cousin. I'm not a hater, so I could admit that Diane was beautiful, but I could also tell she was a weak bitch. I couldn't believe that Chase would even fuck around with someone like that.

Snatching away from the stranger, I turned around, ready to go off, when I got lost in my tracks. The nigga who grabbed me was fine as fuck. I couldn't help but look up at his 6'1 frame towering over me. I admired his creamy, golden, blemish-free skin and fresh fade with waves that could make any bitch seasick. His lips were full and pink, and he had light hazel eyes that I could get lost in. He was built like he'd never missed a day in the gym, and he could bench press me on a bad day. Hearing Shavon groan shook me from my daydream, reminding me why I was so pissed.

"I have to go," I mumbled to the handsome stranger.

He tried to grab me again, but I pushed past him. I rushed back to my job and grabbed my things before storming out. I knew I was about to get fired, but I didn't give a fuck. As I rushed out, I ran right into the sexy stranger again.

"Are you alright, ma? You did a number on ole girl," he stated with a hint of concern.

"I'm fine," I said, keeping it short.

"Okay, well, I'm Blaze. Take my card in case you need anything."

"I'm not interested," I replied.

He grabbed me gently by my arm and stuck his card in my bag before letting me go. I walked away without saying anything. Any other day, I probably would have entertained him, but I was a woman on a mission.

I hopped in my Lexus and drove straight to the trap where I knew Chase was. All I could see was red when I pulled up and saw his car. I jumped out and took the crowbar from my trunk before walking over to Chase's white BMW. I slashed one of his tires with my box cutter, then went to work on the windows with my crowbar.

"What the fuck are you doing?" Chase yelled as he rushed toward me.

I stopped hitting the car and swung on him, catching him right in the shoulder.

"Ouch! What the hell, McKenzie?" Chase groaned in pain.

I was about to swing on his ass again when my brother Tyrese rushed over to me.

"Man, why the fuck you out here showing your ass in front of all these people?" Tyrese shouted.

"Fuck this car and these people. I don't give a fuck about none of them or what they think. And fuck Chase cheating ass too."

"I know you not out here tearing his shit up over no bitch. I told your dumb ass not to fuck with him, but you didn't want to listen. Now you out here heartbroken and looking stupid," Tyrese spat.

I couldn't believe my brother was talking to me like this. In my mind, he was taking Chase's side over mine, and that meant he wasn't loyal. He had me on the verge of tears, but I refused to allow anyone to see them fall. He had just broken my heart more than Chase's deceit.

"Fuck you, Tyrese! I don't give a fuck how many warnings you gave me. You knew he was playing me all this time and didn't say shit. As your little sister, you should be on my side. You should be trying to help me fuck him up instead of trying to kiss his ass. You can keep your bitch ass here with him and don't say shit else to me," I snapped before walking away and climbing in my car.

I drove to my house and went straight to my bedroom. As soon as the door closed, I slid down against it, and my tear dam broke. I released one of the ugliest cries I'd had in a long time. I was beyond crushed by the events that had taken place.

After crying for ten minutes, I got up from the floor and lay in my bed. My tears continued to fall until sleep finally took over.

CHAPTER NINE
CHASE

K.G. was helping me bag some dope when one of my workers rushed in and told me somebody was fucking up my car. I stopped what I was doing and instantly grabbed my gat, ready to shoot someone. When I saw that it was my lil' baby, Kenzie, I was in a state of shock. I had no idea what would possess her to do this. Everything was all good last night when I had her lil' ass screaming my name while I dicked her down all over my house.

I couldn't believe she actually hit me with a crowbar when I tried to stop her. If my car wasn't fucked up, I would have chased after her as soon as she pulled off, but I had to wait an hour for a tow truck. Once it finally came, I filled out the paperwork then climbed in the car with my brother.

"We going to the house to get your other car first?"

"Nah, take me to Kenzie's house, so I can talk to her."

"Don't go over there acting crazy with that girl over that car. What happened anyway? I thought you were with her last night."

"I'm not about to say nothing to her about the car. I can get that shit fixed. I just want to know what I did that made her act like that," I told him.

Tino drove ten minutes until we pulled up to McKenzie's house. He waited in the car while I climbed out to face the music. I rang the doorbell because I knew Kenzie wasn't going to answer the phone. I had already called her about ten times in the past hour.

I waited about a minute before Tyrese opened the door.

"What's up, Ty. Where's your sister?"

"She's in her room. Be careful because she's still pissed, so she might throw something at you."

"It's fine. I can handle her."

I walked to the back and knocked on McKenzie's bedroom door.

"Go away!" she yelled.

I ignored her and opened the door. As soon as I walked in, she grabbed a shoe by her bed and threw it at me. I dodged it, but that didn't stop her from throwing the other shoes next to her bed.

Taking a deep breath, I walked toward McKenzie and grabbed her by the arms.

"What the fuck is wrong with you?" I yelled, allowing my anger to get the best of me.

"You! I told you not to fucking play with me. I asked you nicely before we got together to get rid of your bitches, and you didn't listen. Do you know how fucked up it feels to know that my man has a baby on the way by another bitch?" McKenzie yelled, finally allowing the tears she had been holding to escape her eyes.

"Baby, what are you talking about? I did let everybody go. I don't have nobody pregnant."

"Okay, so who is Diane, Chase?"

McKenzie caught me off guard with that question, but I

couldn't let it show. I had to keep my composure before I gave myself up.

"She's my ex. I don't fuck with her anymore," I said, telling the truth. I hadn't slept under the same roof with Diane since I told her I needed a break two weeks ago. We had barely even talked on the phone during that time because I was wrapped up in work and McKenzie.

"Ex, my ass, Chase! Just get the fuck out if you gon' be lying. That bitch didn't make up being pregnant by you out of nowhere, and I saw her stomach. It doesn't look like she's due any day now, so that means you was fucking with her while we were together. So, answer me this. Which one of us is the side bitch?"

"Man, I don't know shit about that damn girl being pregnant," I stated, avoiding everything else she said.

"Oh, I know you don't. Her and Shavon's dumb ass came to the mall today. While I was on lunch, Shavon had the audacity to throw your bitch's used pregnancy test in my food, talking about, 'since your nigga can't go home, tell him he got a baby on the way.' So, not only were you fucking around with another bitch, but you lived with her. I find that ironic since I was at your house, fucking and sucking you at least four to five times a week. So, I'll ask this again. Which one of us is the side bitch?"

I couldn't believe what I was hearing. The next time I saw Shavon, I was going to fuck her up. I forgot she was cousins with Diane since they weren't around each other often.

"I'm sorry. I swear it's not how it seems. Neither of you was my side bitch. I was with Diane first, but then I fell for you. I tried to find a way to end things with her when me and you got serious, but I didn't know how. I promised her father before he died that I would look after her. Her aunt has stage 4 cancer, so she doesn't have any family. The day I told you I was in love with you, I meant it. I broke things off with her earlier that day before I came over," I explained.

I could have lied, but there was no use at that point. She knew everything already, and if Diane was pregnant, I was truly fucked.

"You son of a bitch. Get the fuck out! We've been together for damn near a year, and you had a girlfriend the entire time? She might not have nobody else, so she needs you, but I damn sure don't," McKenzie shouted as she started punching me and crying.

I stood there and took the hits until it looked like she was hurting her hands, so I grabbed her in my arms and held her tight.

"I'm so sorry, baby. Please tell me how I can fix this. I'm in love with you, not her. I have never felt about her the way I do about you. I need you to tell me how to fix this."

"There is no way for us to fix this when there's a baby involved. I won't be the bitch who stops a child from growing up with a family."

"Look, I don't want to be with Diane. If she's pregnant for real, I'll be there for my baby, but what type of family can I give a child if I'm not happy there?"

McKenzie sighed as she snatched away from me and sat on her bed.

"Not if. I know she's pregnant for real because I saw the damn positive sign. I love you, Chase, but I can't do this with you. I need some time to think because when I look at you now, all I want to do is hit you upside your fucking head. You told me you weren't shit like Chris, and you got a bitch pregnant while we were together too. The only difference in this situation is I'm the side bitch. All you had to do was keep it a buck with me. I told you, in the beginning, we didn't have to be in a relationship to fuck. Hell, who knows? I probably would have still let you hit every now and then if I knew you had a woman, but I wouldn't have been dumb enough to fall in love with your bitch ass."

"I get that you're mad, but watch your fucking mouth before I pop you in it," I warned her.

"I wish the fuck you would try it. They'll be bringing your ass out of here on a stretcher. If you don't like the way I'm talking, you can get your ass out like I been said," she screamed as she jumped in my face.

"Sit your ass down," I snapped before pushing her on her bed and turning to walk away.

"Yeah, run your bitch ass off to your bitch. I hope your dick falls off."

I tried my best to control my anger and walk out until I felt her hit me in the back of my head with something hard. When I turned around, she had a damn trophy in her hand. I grabbed her by her shirt and pushed her against the wall, causing one of her pictures to fall to the floor.

"Stop fucking hitting me before I fuck you up. I'll call you when I think you've calmed down some," I said before releasing her and finally walking out.

I left the house and climbed in Tino's car, trying to maintain my composure. Had this been any other day, I would have fucked McKenzie up for putting her hands on me. She hit me in my shit hard as hell, so I knew I would have a knot on the back of my head.

"You good, Chase?" Tino asked as he pulled off.

"Hell no, take me to the house so I can get my car. I need to go talk to Diane. She let Shavon talk her into some bullshit. Instead of telling me she was pregnant, she decided to give the positive pregnancy test to Kenzie. Now her little ass is out of her body and being disrespectful. I had to leave because I was ready to smack fire from her ass when she hit me in the head with a trophy."

"Damn, that's fucked up," Tino said as he shook his head.

When we pulled up to my house, I saw Diane's car outside. She didn't have keys to my house, so that meant she was in my OG's house with her, and it was really about to be some shit.

I used the key to let myself inside her house and walked into the living room. Diane was sitting on the couch in tears, talking to my momz. As bad as I wanted to get in her ass for that stunt she pulled, I had no right. I was the one in the wrong, and I had hurt her by cheating.

"Hey, son, come in the kitchen and talk to me for a minute," my mother said.

I walked into the kitchen and sat at the table. She pulled out a chair and sat next to me.

"Hey, Ma. What's going on?" I asked.

"Don't come in here talking to me like everything is all good. What have you gotten yourself into with Diane? She's telling me you left her for another woman while she's pregnant. I told you that you needed to figure out what you were going to do months ago when I first met that young ass girl you dealing with."

"It's not like that, Ma. All this time, it feels like I'm with Diane out of obligation because of a promise I made you and her family when we got together. I didn't leave her because she was pregnant. I fell in love with McKenzie and decided to do the right thing and call things off with Diane. I never even knew she was pregnant. Hell, she didn't even tell me. She went to Kenzie's job and told her."

"Okay, she was wrong for that, but at the same time, she's hurt. You need to sit down with her and tell the truth. More importantly, now that she's pregnant again, you need to do what's right and be there for her. You know she's high risk when she's pregnant."

"Let me get this straight. You're telling me that I need to forget about McKenzie and my happiness because Diane is pregnant?" I asked for clarity.

"Yes, at least until after she has the baby. Continue to sneak behind her back with McKenzie if that makes you happy, but you need to take your ass back home with her."

"How can you ask me to do this? Diane got pregnant on purpose. She stopped taking her birth control pills without telling me."

"It doesn't matter. You were still having sex with the girl. Part of being a grown-up is owning up to your responsibilities. You have to put the life of your child over your happiness, and it's as simple as that."

I stood up from the chair and punched a hole in the wall before walking out of the kitchen. As I passed the living room, I stopped and looked at Diane. All I saw was red. I was going to talk to her, but I needed to calm down first, so I walked out of the house, slamming the door. My mama was gon' get in my ass for this stunt, but at that moment, I didn't care.

I walked into my house and poured a drink, then rolled a blunt to help mellow me out. I called Kenzie, and her phone went straight to voicemail, so that meant her ass had blocked me.

In a matter of hours, my world had come crashing down, and I didn't know to fix it. When it was all said and done, I was about to break my baby's heart more because, like my mama said, I had to take care of my responsibilities.

CHAPTER TEN
DIANE

The look Chase gave me before storming out of the house sent chills down my spine. I had never seen him so angry with me in all the time that I'd known him. My first mind was to get my keys and get the hell out of dodge, but there was nowhere for me to run. Chase and his family were the only people who had been in my corner through thick and thin. The only family I had who took care of me when my parents couldn't was my aunt Stacey, and she's in a nursing home now.

All I could do was sit back and watch everything unfold. I brought this shit on myself. I knew the type of guy Chase was when I first laid in bed with him. He was my best friend, and I had never seen him in a real relationship before. He had girls that he had sex with, but he never committed. I thought that with the bond we had, I would be able to change him, so I suggested we start a relationship.

I never thought Chase was an angel. I was sure he cheated on me because he had a higher sex drive than mine, and I didn't give head. It was an out of sight, out of mind situation.

He always found his way home and was respectful of me and my feelings. Chase made sure I felt secure and was well taken care of. He never did anything in my face, and I was never out in the streets fighting over him.

Shavon hit me up about five months ago and told me she heard Chase was fucking with her stepsister. I didn't think anything of it at first. I figured she was just some random female he was using for sex, but then he started changing before my eyes.

Chase started coming in later than usual, and some nights he didn't bother coming in at all. I no longer had his undivided attention. It was like he was there with me physically, but he had checked out mentally. He picked fights with me over the smallest things, just so he would have a reason to not sleep in the bed with me at night.

I caught on really quick to what he was doing and started doing my own research. Chase was never one to be on social media, but I found an Instagram account for him, and it had pictures of him with Kenzie. I was seething with jealousy when I saw that because we never had that. He took me on dates before I moved in, but afterward, they dwindled away. I thought us moving in together would grow us closer, but it only tore us apart.

I could feel my relationship slipping through my fingers. I couldn't lose Chase, so all rational thinking left, and I stopped taking my birth control pills. He didn't want a baby yet, but I didn't care. That was the one thing that would for sure secure my spot in his life for good. He would never turn his back on his child.

The day Chase found my pills, I had already been off them for two months prior. I knew there was a possibility that I was pregnant then. I never meant for him to find out I wasn't on the pill anymore. If I came up pregnant, I was just going to tell him that I missed a day or something. I planned to tell Chase, but after the way he reacted to seeing those pills, I was scared as hell, so I kept my mouth shut and allowed him to walk out.

I went two weeks without seeing Chase, and that shit felt like hell. He still called to check on me and to make sure I didn't need anything, but it wasn't the same. I couldn't tell if I was coming or going. All I did was go to work and back home. To make matters worse, I had missed my period, and I couldn't keep anything down. Shavon was worried, so she came to the house last night, and I broke down. I told her everything, and she convinced me to take a pregnancy test to get it over with.

When it came back positive, I immediately tried calling Chase, but he didn't answer. I knew that meant he was probably with Kenzie. I had finally broken down and started crying. That's when Shavon came up with the idea for us to go tell Kenzie I was pregnant. She said I shouldn't be the only one hurt and that Chase would never tell her about the baby.

I was mad at Chase for not answering me, so I agreed to Shavon's crazy idea. I didn't think about the consequences of our actions. If I could do it all over again, I would change everything. I never would have gotten pregnant on purpose, and I never would have gone to that mall.

The original plan was to go to the Footlocker Kenzie worked at and confront her there. It was just supposed to be a way of embarrassing her. I was going to show her the pregnancy test and tell her to let Chase know, so he could answer, then we were supposed to go on about our way.

We saw her when she sat down for lunch, and I thought it was a bad idea, but Shavon said we could keep the same plan, but the location would just be different. I was baffled when Shavon threw the pregnancy test in Kenzie's food. That was the most disrespectful and nastiest shit I have ever seen. It was no surprise to me when Kenzie jumped up and started beating

Shavon's ass. All I could do was stand there and watch. I'm not a fighter, and I wasn't about to help jump that young ass girl. Her and Shavon were the same age, but I was almost twenty-one years old.

Shavon allowed her own hatred toward Kenzie to get in the way. Working off those emotions is what landed Shavon in the hospital. I had to rush her there after I helped her off the floor. Her nose was broken, she had a black eye, a concussion, and some bruised ribs. I was scared for Shavon's life and mine. I thought Kenzie was going to kill Shavon and then me afterward.

I thanked God above when that man pulled Kenzie off Shavon. He had slowed her down, so she didn't get the chance to attack me. Surprisingly, she never even said anything to me, and that made me feel like shit. Chase was the one I should have confronted, not her.

An hour went by before I heard the front door open and close. I looked up and saw that it was Chase. His eyes were red and low, which indicated that he was faded. I hoped that meant he was finally calm.

"Why didn't you tell me you were pregnant?" Chase asked before sitting down across from me.

"I tried calling you yesterday and today, but you didn't answer."

"That's bullshit, Diane, and you know it. You could have texted and told me it was important. I called you two days ago to check on you, and you didn't say shit. I'm sure you knew your ass was pregnant before yesterday. What would even possess you to go confront that girl? You should have come to me if you found out I was fucking around with her. This is all on me. I owed you loyalty, not her."

"I know, but at the same time, I didn't want to be the only one hurt. I couldn't believe you started another relationship while you were with me. Y'all was out here bold, like you didn't have someone at home waiting on you."

Chase sighed and wiped his hand across his face.

"It wasn't like that, Diane. I didn't know how to break things off without hurting you. McKenzie didn't know about you, though. She's innocent in this situation. As far as she knew, she was my one and only girl because that's how I treated her. I fucked up, and my selfishness hurt both of you."

I debated on asking the million-dollar question that I yearned to know the answer to.

"Do you love her?"

"Yes, but I can't be with her anymore. I'm going to do the right thing and be here for you and our unborn child," he replied with no hesitation.

I had to admit a piece of my heart broke when he said he loved another woman, but I kept it together.

"How long were you two together?" I asked.

"Does it matter? I just told you that I was going to end things with her and stay with you."

"Yes, it matters. We need to clear the air if we're going to be together."

"We were together for about nine months."

"Okay, it's going to take some time for me to trust you again, but I forgive you. I love you, Chase, and nothing can change that."

"I love you too. Do you have a doctor's appointment scheduled yet?"

"No, I just took the test yesterday."

"Alright, we can call Monday to schedule it."

"So, are you coming home with me tonight, or you need to go make things right with little Miss Kenzie."

"Come on, Diane, we not about to start this shit. How you gon' say you forgive me five seconds ago but then bring Kenzie up? If this is what it's going to be like, then we can just co-parent. I got too much shit going on to have to deal with this. I literally just told you I was going to leave her alone. That girl doesn't want nothing to do with me. Go home, and I'll be there in a couple hours. I have some work to finish."

"Okay, I need to go check on Shavon first. Kenzie beat her up and put her in the hospital."

"That's what the fuck she gets for starting shit. I know you wouldn't have done any of that if it wasn't for her."

I went upstairs to let his mom know I was leaving, then I left the house and went back to the hospital.

CHAPTER ELEVEN
MCKENZIE

This morning, I woke up to loud arguing. I looked over at the clock and saw it was 4:55 a.m. I was not in the mood for this shit, especially since I only had about three hours of sleep. Yesterday, after Chase left, I drowned my sorrows with a bottle of tequila, and now I was going to pay for it.

"Where the hell have you been all night?" my mother yelled.

"I told you I was going to check on my daughter," my step-father, Rick, yelled back.

"I'm not trying to hear that shit. That was fourteen hours ago. It doesn't take that long to check on your daughter. I counted your blue pills, and there are two missing. I know your broke ass can't afford to be cheating when you can't even afford to pay a bill," my mother snapped.

"Celeste, shut the fuck up and get out of my face before I beat your ass. My daughter is in the hospital because of your damn daughter. McKenzie better watch her back because I'm not taking this shit lightly."

"You know better than to threaten my daughter. If she did something to Shavon, then I'm sure it was Shavon's fault, so I advise you to stay away from my child. You and me both know you don't want those problems."

"You just don't know when to shut the fuck up. I guess you gon' take this ass whooping instead," Rick bellowed.

I heard my mom scream, which caused me to jump out of bed. When I made it out of my room, my mother was on the floor, holding her face and crying with Rick hovering over her, sending blows to her body.

"Get the fuck away from my mama!" I yelled at Rick as I pushed him off her.

"Stay out of it, Kenzie. It's alright, baby. Go back to your room," my mom ordered.

"Yeah, listen to your mother, or you're next. All of this is your fault anyway. You nearly killed my damn daughter!" Rick shouted.

"Be glad the bitch ain't dead. Next time, she'll think twice before fucking with me," I snapped.

"You bitch! I'm going to beat your ass like my daughter should have." Rick charged toward me and put his hand around my neck, pushing me into the wall.

My mother jumped up from the floor and tried to grab his arms, but he was too strong. He flung her off him while one hand remained around my neck, choking the life out of me. I could smell the alcohol on his breath, and it had me ready to vomit.

"Rick, stop! You're hurting her," my mother pleaded through tears.

I dug my fingernails into Rick's hand, trying to relieve some of the pressure, but it didn't faze him one bit.

"Yo, what the fuck is going on in here?" Tyrese yelled as he rushed over to us and pushed Rick off me. So much was going on that none of us heard him come in.

I bent over and held my knees, trying to catch my breath as tears fell from my eyes. Once I got my breath regulated, I wiped my tears and walked back into my room. I grabbed my steel bat and returned to the living room, where Rick was talking to my mother.

I swung the bat and hit Rick in the back with all my might, causing him to fall over. I swung again and hit him in his arm, then again in his legs. My mother was screaming my name, but I had blacked out for the second time in twenty-four hours. I couldn't believe this man had just tried to kill me and was still in this house.

"You're going to kill him! Kenzie, please stop," my mother begged. I couldn't believe she had the audacity to try to stop me when he had just beat her ass and choked me up.

"What the fuck? Kenz, stop," Tyrese bellowed as he pulled me off of Ricky.

I turned around and slapped the shit out of Tyrese.

"That's the second time you chose somebody over me. I told you to stay the fuck away from me," I said through gritted teeth before walking to my bedroom and slamming the door.

I couldn't stay in that house any longer. I pulled out my phone and called the one person I always dialed when I was having a crisis or meltdown.

"Hello," Martez answered groggily.

"Hey, I can't do this anymore," I cried into the phone.

"What's wrong, Kenz? Do I need to get on a plane?" Martez asked, clearer this time.

"No, I need to get away. Everything is just all bad right now. I'm going to end up in jail if I stay in Chicago or in this house another day." I cried even harder.

My heart was broken, and there was nothing I could do

about it. Everyone chose to break me at once, and there was only so much I could do on my own. I had no fight in me, and there was no way in hell I could stay in that house if Rick was still going to be there.

"I need you to stop crying and tell me what's going on, so I can help you. I can't help you, baby girl, if you don't tell me what's wrong," he calmly said.

I took a deep breath and told Martez everything that had transpired from the fight at the mall until now. I made sure not to leave out anything. It felt good to finally get everything off my chest. I hadn't told anyone what happened between Chase and me because I had powered my phone off and locked myself in my bedroom. I brushed everyone off and stayed to myself. Aniyah had stayed with Charmaine last night, which was a good thing.

"I'm about to get up now and hop on a plane. I'm about to fuck them all up," Martez growled.

I could hear shuffling and his fiancée, Lauren, talking in the background, so I knew that meant he was getting out of bed.

"No, that's not going to solve anything, Martez. I need to get out of here and away from everybody. Please talk to Daddy because I don't want to explain everything all over again, but maybe leave the Chase part out."

"Okay, so what do you want to do, Kenzie? We can't find you a house overnight. You know it's going to take time for me to come up there and find you something."

"I don't care about that right now. Can I just come stay with y'all?"

"Of course. You know you're welcome here. I'll talk to Dad, and he can let your mother know. You can't just skip town without telling her."

"Alright, so what should I do?"

"Pack whatever you'll need to bring here, and I'll book you a flight, then text you the itinerary."

"Thank you, Martez. I love you so much."

"I love you too, baby girl," he replied before hanging up.

I grabbed my carry-on suitcase from my closet and started packing things that I might need. I didn't know how long I would be gone, but I had more than enough clothes in Miami. As I was zipping my suitcase, my mother knocked on my door before walking in.

"Hey, I just got off the phone with your father. You don't have to leave, Kenzie. Rick will leave you alone. He was drunk and didn't mean any harm."

I snapped my neck in the direction of my mother so fast I almost caught whiplash.

"How can you stand here and tell me he didn't mean any harm? He was literally hitting on you and then choked me up. I don't care how drunk he is. He doesn't get a pass for that. I know that's not the first time he's put his hands on you, but it was the first and last time he'll ever get a chance to put them on me. I just had to talk Martez out of hopping on a plane to come here. So, as long as your husband is living here, I can't."

"Okay, I'll call and tell your father it's alright for you to come." She sighed.

"Thank you," I said before turning back around to finish closing my suitcase.

My mother walked out of my room in defeat. Five minutes later, there was a text from my brother.

#1 Big Bro: They have a 9:00 flight. Is that too early?"

Me: No, I'm already done packing, so I'll make it to the airport in time.

#1 Big Bro: Okay, me or Lauren will be there to pick you up.

Me: See you soon!

I put my phone back in my purse and debated on if I should

call my sister and let her know I was leaving. If I told her, she would tell Quan, and I didn't want Chase to know before I left, so I shook the idea away and called Tori instead.

"Hello," Tori answered.

"Hey, I know it's early, but I need a huge favor. Can you drop me off at the airport, and I'll leave my car with you?"

"Of course. I'll throw on some clothes now."

"Thank you so much. I'll be there in thirty minutes," I said before hanging up.

I went into the bathroom and freshened up, then put on a PINK jogging suit and a pair of socks with my slides. I didn't like wearing gym shoes to the airport because it was too much hassle taking my shoes off and putting them back on.

After grabbing my suitcase, backpack, and purse, I walked out of my bedroom. My mother was sitting on the couch with her face in her hands, and Tyrese was sitting next to her.

"My flight is at nine, so I'm about to leave now so Tori can drop me off," I said, causing my mom to look up.

I saw the tears in her eyes, and I felt bad because I knew I was partially responsible for them, but I couldn't stay.

"Okay, call me when you land," she replied.

I walked over to my mother and squatted down so I could hug her.

"I will. I love you, Ma," I told her before kissing her on the forehead.

"I love you too, baby."

I stood up and walked toward the front door. Tyrese called my name, but I ignored him. I was serious when I told him to stay away from me.

"McKenzie, I know you hear me," he shouted as he pulled me by my arm.

I looked down at his hand and snatched away.

"Keep your hands to yourself," I stated through clenched teeth.

"You're just going to leave, Kenzie? This is so selfish of you. Do you not realize how you're hurting Ma? You're not innocent in this situation. Had you not been out there fighting over a nigga, none of this would be happening."

"First of all, you don't know what the hell you're talking about. I didn't fight Shavon over a nigga. I beat her ass for disrespecting me. The bitch threw a pissy pregnancy test in my food. Second of all, I wasn't about to just sit here and listen to him beat Ma's ass, and I damn sure wasn't going to allow him to choke me and get away with it. I'm glad I'm finally seeing this side of you. I knew that you favored Aniyah over me, and it's finally showing."

"What? Kenzie, that's not even true."

"It is, but it's all good because I have another brother who loves me and will always have my back," I said on the verge of tears before walking down the stairs and to my car.

I climbed in my car and drove the ten minutes it took to get to Tori's house. I called to let her know I was outside, and she came out five minutes later.

"Hey, best friend, where are you going?" Tori asked.

"I'm going to Miami to stay with Martez and my father. I don't know how long I'll be there yet."

"Is everything alright?"

"No, everything is all bad."

I replayed the same events to Tori that I did to Martez during the drive to the airport.

"I'm so sorry, Kenzie. Is there anything I can do for you?"

"No, I just need to get away and think. Ask your parents if it's alright for me to leave my car in your garage until I can figure out what to do with it. If not, leave it in your driveway. Don't give my keys to my brother or sister."

"Alright, I got you."

We had basic girl talk for the remainder of the drive until I pulled up at the airport.

"Take care of my car. I'll call you when I land."

"Okay, babez, be safe."

I got out of the car, grabbed my things from the trunk, and walked through the airport, headed straight to the TSA presecurity check-in. I was glad it wasn't crowded because I didn't feel like standing in a long line. Once I finished, I looked for my gate and sat down. I only had about thirty minutes before they called my boarding number.

It was a last-minute flight, but Martez was able to get me a first-class ticket, so I wasn't stuck in the back of the plane or in a middle seat. I found my seat and put my headphones on, ready to sleep for the rest of the flight.

Once I landed in Miami, Lauren picked me up from the airport and took me to the house. My father and brother were away in meetings, so I went straight to my room and locked myself inside.

CHAPTER TWELVE
BLAZE

"Oh, shit, Kim, I'm about to nut," I announced before busting down her throat.

She looked up at me with her brown doe eyes and smiled as she swallowed every drop. I pushed her hair out of her face and kissed her on the forehead before getting up from the couch. Then, I walked into the bathroom and climbed into the shower with her following me. She dropped to her knees and sucked my dick until I was hard in her mouth. I had a meeting to get to with a new connect, so I didn't have time to play with her all evening.

I lifted her up and bent her over the tub before plunging into her from the back. I beat her pussy up for fifteen minutes before nutting on her back. After we finished, we showered and got out. I looked in my suitcase and grabbed a pair of boxers along with some black jeans, a white t-shirt, and a pair of black and white Giuseppe sneakers. Once I was dressed, I squirted on my Versace Eros cologne and put on my jewelry. I took my wave cap off and brushed my hair, then grabbed my phone from the dresser.

"I don't see why I can't go with you," Kim pouted.

"I told you when you asked to come out here with me that this wasn't just a leisure trip. I have business to handle while I'm here and an event with my family. I took you out yesterday and this morning. Now it's time for me to take care of business. I'll probably be back late, so don't wait up."

"Fine. I guess I'll watch TV and order room service," she mumbled.

I grabbed my keys and wallet then walked out of the room, ignoring her attitude. She was the one who begged to come out here with me since she needed to get away. Kim had never been my girlfriend, and she never would be. I brought her because she was cool to hang with and bomb on the head.

I met Kim last year at a strip club. She was a dark-skinned beauty with a big ass, thick thighs, and wide hips. I couldn't keep my eyes off her while she was out on the dance floor, so I paid her for a lap dance, then we exchanged numbers. I took her out to dinner, and we went to the hotel right after. We went on a few dates after that and continued to fuck, but I never got the feeling of wanting to make her my woman.

Kim was a cool, down to earth girl, but we only connected sexually. She was more like a homegirl that I fucked around with. She was allowed to do whatever she wanted with whoever she wanted, and so was I. I used her to make runs with me sometimes or set niggas up if one of my other female workers wasn't available.

I climbed in my rental, put the address in my GPS, and drove off. The house was about thirty minutes from the hotel where I was staying. When I pulled up, I had to check in with security before they opened the gate. I drove for almost five minutes until I pulled up to a big ass mansion off the ocean. I drove up the long driveway and parked. There were all types of foreign cars parked in the driveway. This house was some big boy shit.

I was a twenty-four-year-old paid nigga, so I was used to expensive shit, but this was on an entirely different level. In a couple more years, I would be ready to settle down and get a house like this for my kids and future wife.

I got in the game when I was eighteen years old after my father died. He left everything to my big brother Mason and me. Mason lived in Cali, and I expanded our business to Chicago while taking college classes. We sold weapons, any drugs you could think of, and we had legit businesses in Cali, Miami, and Chicago.

I got out of the car and rang the doorbell. After about two minutes, the door swung open to a smiling Lauren.

"Hey, cousin," she beamed.

"Hey, lil' girl. How are you?"

"Shut up. You must've forgotten that I'm older than you."

"I don't care. You'll always be little," I told her.

Lauren rolled her eyes and stepped out of the way, allowing me to enter. I followed her to an office, where she knocked lightly before pushing the door open.

"Hey, baby. Can you go check on my sister while I have this meeting with your cousin?" Martez asked.

"Okay. I'm going to try and get her to come out of her room," Lauren replied.

"What's up, Tez," I spoke before sitting down across from him.

"What's going on, Blaze? You ready to get down to business?"

"Yeah, I'm looking to cop thirty bricks at twenty-three a pop, and I have the blueprints for the house you asked for."

"Good looking out. How long are you in town for?"

"I'm here for the week."

"Cool, I'll arrange for the drugs to get to Chicago by the time you make it back, and I'll go over the blueprints and send them back with you."

"Do you plan on moving to Chicago or something?"

"No, sir, my sister lives out there. It's a late birthday gift to her."

Martez and I talked about business for another thirty minutes before we left his office. I followed him to the living room, where a group of guys was sitting around drinking. He introduced me to them and then handed me a bottle of Patrón and a glass. I poured a shot and knocked it back before pouring another one.

"Martez, Papa wants you. He's in the kitchen," a female voice said from behind me.

I turned around and couldn't believe my eyes. It was the girl I met at the mall in Chicago a couple weeks ago. I never forgot a face, and I definitely would never forget the face of the one female I gave my number to who never used it. I didn't believe in coincidences, but I did believe in fate.

She wasn't as thick as the women I typically went after, but she was drop-dead gorgeous with a fit body that turned heads. Her naturally curly hair was pulled up into a ponytail, and she wore a half shirt that showed off her flat stomach and diamond belly ring with a short pair of biker shorts.

"Damn, that's Martez lil' sister?" one of the guys asked, causing the girl to roll her eyes.

"McKenzie, go put on some clothes," Martez told her.

"No. It's not my fault that your friends are creeps. I'm not paying attention to any of them anyway, and it's not like I'm about to stay in here with y'all. I only came to grab something and tell you Papa wanted you," she replied.

McKenzie locked eyes with me and winked before walking over to the bar. She grabbed a bottle of tequila and a shot glass before walking back out of the living room. I sat with the guys for about twenty minutes until Lauren came in and sat by me.

"Hey, cousin, sorry I'm not keeping you much company. I was sitting out on the deck, talking to Tez's sister, trying to convince her not to go back to her room."

"It's cool. Your man and his friends are not a bad crowd to hang with. They're talking about going out to the club, so I'll probably go with them, but what's going on with his lil' sister?"

"Why? Are you interested? I talked to her about you yesterday and told her you'd be here."

"I actually met her before. I broke up a fight she had in the mall back home. I gave her my card, and she never called me. Does she live out there or here?"

"I don't really know the answer to that right now. You would have to ask her, but she's been out here since that fight. She hasn't said if or when she's going back to Chicago. It's not my place to tell you what's going on with her, but you can go out back with me to talk to her if you want to. I can't guarantee that she'll talk back, though."

"She will," I said with confidence.

I got up from the couch and followed Lauren through the house until we made it to the back. There was a large patio fully decked out with furniture and a huge pool that was surrounded by a lawn and a deck that led to the ocean behind it. Slow jams played back there that couldn't be heard in the front of the house. McKenzie was sitting on one of the chairs in a corner, drinking her tequila and smoking.

"Kenz, this is my cousin Blaze. Blaze, this is McKenzie."

"Hey," she said without looking up.

"Hey, beautiful," I said before pulling out the chair and sitting next to her.

She sighed before looking up at me.

"How can I help you?" she asked with irritation in her voice.

"You're too beautiful to always be so angry. Do you remember me?"

"Yeah, you're the one who stopped me from killing that dumb bitch in the mall."

"Why didn't you call me? I gave you my card."

"You told me to call you if I needed you, and I didn't." She shrugged before taking another shot.

I took the bottle from her and slid it out the way.

"How old are you?" I asked.

"No, we're not about to do this. I wasn't interested when you gave me your number in the mall, and I'm not interested now."

I sat back in my seat and looked into her eyes. I could tell from the sadness I saw that she'd been hurt recently, so that meant I would have to go about this a different way. I would have to be patient and take things slow.

"Come on, I'm not asking for your hand in marriage. I'm just asking you to let me take you out to dinner."

"Look, no offense... you seem like a decent guy, but I'm over the male species, and I'm sure I won't be much company."

I wasn't about to bow out so easily. I needed to take my shot while I could because it was no telling when I would see or talk to her again if I gave up and walked away now.

"It's just dinner, and you have to eat. We can go anywhere you want as friends. We don't even have to call it a date. We can sit down, and you can tell me all about your problems. It might help to talk to a stranger with an unbiased opinion."

McKenzie got quiet and sat back, momentarily giving some thought to what I said before speaking.

"Is Blaze your real name?" she asked, catching me off guard.

I didn't typically tell strangers my real name, but I'd make an exception for her.

"No, it's Malakai, but everyone calls me Blaze. Now, will you let me take you out to dinner?" I couldn't believe I was actually going through all of this just to get someone to go out with me.

"How long are you in town for?" she asked.

"I'll be here until Sunday."

"Okay, if you ask my brother, and he approves, then I'll go, but it's not a date. I'm not interested in dating anyone right now."

"Alright, I don't have a problem with that. I was going to talk to Tez anyway since I do business with him." I wanted to get to know Kenzie, but at the same time, I didn't want to fuck up my business behind her.

"773-277-4122. You can pick the time and place. Text me the details, Malakai," she said before getting up and walking away.

All I could do was shake my head. I could already tell this girl was a piece of work. If only she knew I was going to make her pay for all this later, once I cracked her shell.

I walked back into the house and to the living room.

"Tez, can I holler at you for a minute in private before we leave?"

Tez got up and walked into the dining room, and I followed him.

"You want to take my sister out, don't you?"

"How did you know?"

"I asked Lauren where you were, and she said you was outside talking to Kenzie. I don't care if you take her because I can't say who she can and can't date. She's nineteen now, so I can only allow her to make her own decisions. If it was up to me, my sister would be single forever. I do have to warn you, though, that my sister is a handful. Don't let that innocent look fool you."

"Believe me, I already know that. I was the one who broke her fight up at the mall and just spent the past twenty minutes trying to convince her to go out with me, only for her to agree but point out that it's not a date."

"She'll come around eventually. Right now, the timing is just off. All I can say is, be patient if you want to get to know her for real."

"I'm already seeing that. I'll text her and let her know you said it was cool."

I had a few more drinks with the guys before we left and went to the club.

CHAPTER THIRTEEN
MCKENZIE

"TT, wake up. TT, wake up now," my niece McKenna screamed as she bounced on top of me.

"McKenna, get up off me, little girl," I mumbled.

When she didn't move, I fluttered my eyes open, flipped her on her back, then tickled her until she started laughing uncontrollably.

"I'm sorry! You're going to make me pee. Papa told me to do it." McKenna giggled.

I sat up in bed and pulled my five-year-old niece on my lap. I looked down at her and smiled warmly. When she was born, my brother said she looked like me, so he gave her a name close to mine. She had the same light caramel complexion with brown, almond shaped eyes, curly hair, and deep dimples. It's amazing how DNA works. My father has some strong ass genes. Even though Martez and I have different mothers, we looked just alike. I was just a shade lighter than him.

My father got Martez's mother pregnant when she was seventeen years old. She never wanted him, but my father didn't believe in abortions, so she had Martez and signed over her rights to my father. With the help of his parents and a nanny, they raised Martez. He searched for his mother once he was older and found out she died from a drug overdose.

"What does your Papa want, Kenna?"

"I don't know." She shrugged before jumping off the bed.

I looked over at the clock and saw that it was already 10:30 a.m. I groaned, then leaned over and grabbed my phone. I saw that there was a text from Malakai.

Malakai: *I'll be there at 7 to get you, so be ready, or you're going in whatever you have on.*

Me: *Okay, daddy *insert sarcasm**

Malakai: *Look at you, ready to call me daddy already.*

Me: *You wish.*

Malakai: *I'm a very patient man. You might not be ready to call me daddy now, but you will eventually.*

Me: *Sure, I'm going back to sleep. I'll be ready when you get here.*

I placed my phone back on my nightstand and smiled lightly before closing my eyes. As much as I didn't want to like Malakai, he seemed cool, but there was no way in hell I was about to rush into anything with another man. If I've learned anything from the two relationships I've been in, it's that a man will show you the side he wants you to see, and the other side will sneak out when you least expect it. I wanted to think he might be different since he was Lauren's cousin, and she's a sweetheart. She and my brother had been together for six years, and I loved her like a sister. I couldn't wait until they got married next year.

Over the past three days, Malakai would text me good morning and to see how I was doing. Neither of us had really told each other anything personal yet. I guess we were both saving it for tonight when we went on our date that wasn't a date. He'd been by the house every day to either handle business with Martez or to see Lauren and Mckenna. The first day he came, I was in my room and didn't feel like coming out, then the next day, my father dragged me to one of his business meetings.

I didn't see him until yesterday because Lauren's slick ass tricked me, which was probably courtesy of Malakai. I promised my niece I would go to Miami Seaquarium with them, and when we got there, Malakai was waiting for us. We made small talk throughout the day, but it was nothing major. He was very attentive with McKenna, which made me think he had kids. I'd have to find out ages and the story behind that before I even attempted anything with him because we all know how niggas love they baby mama.

I didn't realize I had fallen back to sleep until my brother was standing over me, yelling my name.

"McKenzie, wake up," Martez yelled.

"What do you want, Martez? It's too early for all this yelling." I groaned as I rolled over and pulled the cover over my head.

"It's not early. It's almost two, McKenzie. Get out of this bed," he ordered before pulling the blanket off me.

"What do you want?" I yelled.

"Here, get up," he said and passed me a bag.

I opened the bag and dumped the contents out onto my bed.

"I know you didn't wake me up for this. What the hell am I supposed to do with a pregnancy test?" I asked.

"You're going to get your ass out of bed and go take it."

"Why am I taking this? What makes you think I'm pregnant?"

"You've been throwing up off and on since you've been here, barely eating and staying in bed unless someone makes you get up. Those are the same symptoms Lauren had when she was pregnant."

"I've been throwing up because I've been drinking a lot. I've been in bed because I've been depressed, and I've been sleeping because I'm not in the mood for anything. My life is fucking falling apart."

"Watch your damn mouth, McKenzie. And if that's the case, then there's nothing wrong with you taking the test to prove me wrong unless you're going to sit here and tell me that you weren't having sex with him."

I sighed and got out of bed. There was no use in lying to Martez because he was far from stupid, and I was always open with him regarding my relationships. I grabbed the pregnancy test and went to the bathroom. I peed on the stick, then brushed my teeth and washed my face since I had to wait three minutes.

I picked up the pregnancy test, and my eyes grew big as saucers. Then I sat on the edge of the tub and tried to think back to my last period. I came on last month, but I only spotted for a couple days. I didn't think anything of it since my period is irregular. Tears instantly welled up in my eyes. I couldn't believe I was actually pregnant. I wiped my eyes and grabbed the test, then went back into my bedroom.

I sat on the bed next to Martez and showed him the results.

"You were right. What am I going to do? I can't have this baby!" I cried.

Martez pulled me close and consoled me until I calmed down, then he let me go.

"I know you don't want to hear this, but Dad and I both warned you about the consequences of sex and what would happen if you got pregnant. You're going to have this baby, McKenzie, because you laid there, knowing what could happen. You know Dad doesn't believe in abortion, and neither do I. You don't have to do it on your own because Lauren, Dad, and I will help you no matter what. If you decide to go back to Chicago, I will go down there and help you find a house for you and the baby. If you decide to stay here, that's fine too. There's more than enough room, and you can still have your privacy."

"I can't think about any of that right now. This is so fucked up, Tez. I'm not even on speaking terms with Chase right now."

"I know, baby girl, but you to have to tell him. He has a right to be in his child's life."

"I know. How am I going to tell Papa? He's going to be so disappointed in me."

"He loves you, and he's not going to be disappointed. He'll probably be a little upset because you didn't wait longer, but you're nineteen and have a good head on your shoulders. I mean, he knows better than anyone how unexpected pregnancy can be. If it was always in our control, neither you nor I would be here."

"I love you. You're the best big brother in the world."

"I love you too, sis. Now, get up and go shower, then we can talk to Dad together."

I went in the bathroom and climbed into the shower. My conversation with Martez was heavy on my mind.

Martez was right about the space and privacy part. My father had the master suite downstairs. My brother was on the East with two bedrooms, and I was on the West with two bedrooms and a gym. There was also a guest cottage with two bedrooms on the property as well. It was too soon for me to figure out whether I wanted to live here or in Chicago, though. As much as I didn't want anything to do with Chase, I would have to reach out to him and let him know I was pregnant.

After my shower, I got dressed in a pair of leggings and a

half-shirt before going down to talk to my father. I walked into the living room, and he was sitting on the couch with Martez.

"Hey, Papa, I need to talk to you about something."

"Hey, princess, why do you look so sad?"

"I'm so sorry. I should have been more careful. I'm pregnant," I said and broke down crying all over again.

"Come here, mija. It's okay, you don't have to apologize to me," my dad told me as he pulled me in his arms and rocked me back and forth. He kissed me on the forehead and held me for what felt like an eternity.

I stayed downstairs and talked to my brother and father for a little while, then went to the kitchen and ate some fruit. After that, I went back up to my room and sent Malakai a text to cancel our date. There was no point in me getting to know him. I was pregnant, and no man would want to get to know a pregnant woman with as much baggage as I had.

* * *

I spent the rest of the day sulking in my bedroom after I talked to my father. I had so much shit going on in my head and decisions to make, but I didn't know where to start. Malakai didn't text me back after I canceled, and I can't lie; I kind of felt some kind of way about that. I thought he would have at least asked why. I guess he finally realized that I wasn't worth the trouble.

"Kenzie, can I come in?" Lauren asked.

"Yeah," I replied.

"I know you want to be left alone, but Blaze is here, and he's not leaving until you come down to see him."

"Why? I sent him a message earlier letting him know I needed to cancel."

"I don't know, Kenzie. You have to go talk to him yourself. He's not telling me anything."

I sighed, then climbed out of bed and followed Lauren down the stairs. When I walked into the living room, Malakai was sitting on the couch, scrolling through his phone. When he saw me, he put it away and stood up from the couch.

"Come take a walk with me," Malakai said.

"Malakai, I sent you a message and canceled. Did you not get it?"

"Yeah, I got it, but I told you that I was coming no matter what. We don't have to go out anywhere. I just want to sit down and talk with you."

I could tell Malakai wasn't going to take no for an answer, so I went up to my room and put on my hoodie. I walked back downstairs and led Malakai out to the back of my house and onto the deck. The view of the ocean was breathtaking, and the smell was intoxicating. I loved the smell of the ocean. That's why I slept with the door on my balcony open at night.

We sat in silence for a few minutes before Malakai finally broke it.

"Why did you cancel on me all of a sudden? We talked this morning, and everything was all good."

"You seem like a good guy and someone I would be lucky to know, but my life is so fucked up right now, and I can't bring myself to get you caught up in it."

"I'm a grown man. Give me a chance to decide on what I can and can't handle. I told you that I wanted to get to know you. I'm not trying to rush you into anything. I knew from the first time I gave you my number that you were not ready for a relationship. So, tell me what's going on with you. I can probably help."

"Okay, long story short, the day you saw me at the mall fighting, the girl told me that my boyfriend had got her cousin pregnant. I didn't fight her over him. I fought her because she threw a pregnancy test in my food. After that, I went and fucked his car up, then went home. The next day, some shit went down with my mom and stepfather, and I ended up beating him with a bat. I was starting to spiral out of control, so that's when I came here to get away. Just when it felt like things couldn't get any worse for me, they did. I took a pregnancy test this morning and found out I was pregnant. Now I need to decide on if I want to stay here or go back to Chicago to raise my child."

"Damn, did you talk to your boyfriend about any of this?"

"He's my ex, and no. I haven't talked to him since he tried to explain what was going on."

"You need to talk to him, especially since you're pregnant. You can't run away from your problems. It's not good for your mental or physical health. I'm not telling you that you need to move back to Chicago, but dude has a right to be in his child's life."

"I know you're right, but I don't know where to start. What if I go back there, and he acts crazy or doesn't want my child? Then I'll be stuck there, raising a baby on my own with all my support out here."

"I'm a patient man when it's something I really want. I'm not going to start anything with you while you're pregnant because you need time to heal from your past relationship. I know it's a package deal if I want to be with you. You won't be raising your child on your own in Chicago whether the father is there or not. I'm going to be your friend, so I'll be there for you and the baby. I have to make sure that nigga is completely out of your system before we cross that friendship line because I don't plan on sharing you."

I was shocked by Malakai's response. That answer is not what I expected from him. I just knew he would run for the hills after finding out I was pregnant.

"Thank you for being so understanding. Do you have any kids?"

"Yeah, I have a five-year-old son and a two-year-old daughter."

"You're not with either of the kids' mothers?"

"No, I was in a relationship with my son's mother, but she didn't like the fast life I was living, so we broke up. The traveling between Chicago, Miami, and Cali was too much for our relationship, and she ended up falling for somebody else. She's actually married now to the guy. My other baby mama is a girl I was fucking around with, and the condom broke.

"Do you have any siblings?"

"I have an older brother and younger sister who lives in LA. We were born and raised in Compton until my father started making real money, then moved us to LA. I stayed there until I was eighteen, then I moved to Chicago."

Malakai and I stayed outside talking for almost three hours, just getting to know each other. I could actually see myself falling for him one day because he was down to earth and easy to talk to. I needed to talk to Chase and try to fix everything going on in my life first, so I could be mentally prepared for a man like Malakai.

I let Malakai out through the front, then went upstairs to my room and took a quick shower before getting in bed. For the first time in the past two weeks, I went to sleep with a smile on my face and was able to see the brighter side of life, and it was all because of Malakai.

CHAPTER FOURTEEN
MCKENZIE

5 MONTHS LATER

It's amazing how much your life can change in a matter of months. My trip to Miami was exactly what I needed. I was able to clear my head, and I started taking online classes at the University of Phoenix. I felt way better than I had in a while, and I was focused on me and getting my life together. After I got over the shock of being pregnant, Lauren helped me find an OB-GYN. I found out at my first appointment that I was already eight weeks pregnant with twins. Now, at seven months, it was by the grace of God that my kids were doing well, considering the way I was drinking at the beginning of my pregnancy.

As much as I loved being in Miami, I had just landed back in Chicago. My father and brother wanted me to stay out there until I gave birth, but I felt like I had run away from my problems long enough. If I waited any longer, my doctor wouldn't approve of me flying. I had my medical records transferred and scheduled an ultrasound and appointment with my new OB-GYN. It was a lot that I needed to do before the twins got here, and I still didn't know what I was having yet. I wanted to give Chase the option of being present when I found out.

I didn't want him to have to travel back and forth for appointments, and as much as my parents made it seem easy raising me with them living in different states, I didn't want that for my kids. Even if we couldn't be in the same house, I at least wanted to be a car ride away if something happened.

"How are we getting to the hotel?" I asked Martez.

"Blaze is outside waiting for us already," he replied.

We went to baggage claim to get our luggage and headed outside. Malakai's fine ass was leaning against his black Bentley Bentayga.

"Hey, beautiful," Malakai spoke as he pulled me into his arms.

"Hey, handsome," I replied.

It felt like I could melt in his arms. His Bond No.9 cologne instantly hit my nostrils, and my panties moistened. This man did something to me every time I saw him. I hated to admit it, but I missed him. I hadn't seen him since last month.

Ever since the day Malakai and I spent time together on the deck of my house, we'd grown close. Before I came back out here, he came and visited me a few times. He and Martez took turns going to my doctor's appointments with me. Malakai had been a very good friend to me. We didn't have the brother and sister vibe because the chemistry and sexual attraction were there, but we agreed to wait until after I had the kids before we entertained the idea of getting together. If I wasn't pregnant, I would have given in by now and started a relationship with him. I'd be bouncing on that dick morning, noon, and night.

"Okay, y'all missed each other, now get in the car. It's fucking cold out here. I don't know how y'all deal with this damn weather," Martez complained.

"Stop being a baby. It's not even that bad." I laughed.

It was November, and the weather was fifty-five degrees. That was actually decent weather in Chicago for this time of year.

"Shit, I was just outside without a jacket on in Miami," Martez replied.

I ignored him and pulled out my phone to text Tori and let her know I was back in town.

We drove for about thirty minutes until Malakai pulled up to a beautiful two-story townhome. The house was made of brick, and everything looked brand new. The lawn was perfectly manicured, like it was just cut. I wondered what we were doing there because I expected us to go straight to the hotel, so I could relax. Carrying two little humans was no joke. My feet and back were starting to ache just from sitting in the car.

"Malakai, what are we doing here? I thought you were taking us to the hotel and looking at houses tomorrow."

"There's been a change of plans. Now, stop asking questions and get out of the car," he said.

We all got out, and Malakai typed in a code on the lockbox to get the key. He opened the door, and I was surprised to see the house fully furnished already.

The first floor had an open concept with smoky brown wood floors, vaulted ceilings, and oversized windows to let natural light in. The living room was decorated in red, black, and silver. There was a black leather sectional with an ottoman and chaise. Red and silver decorative pillows were on the couch, and there was a plush black area rug in the center of the floor with a glass coffee table. A sixty-five-inch TV was mounted on the wall over a brick-faced wood-burning fireplace.

The dining area had a tall black table with chairs and a black China cabinet stocked with dishes. A glass sliding door led to a private patio. The kitchen had black and white granite counters, stainless steel appliances, and a large island for seating with bar stools. There were two pantry closets and off-white maple cabinets with crown molding. Silver and black appliances were on the counters. A bedroom and half bathroom were right off the kitchen as well, and the backyard was huge with a gazebo.

Downstairs featured a finished full basement with a laundry room, full bath, bedroom, office, and rec area. There was also a wet bar, extra refrigerator, and storage.

The second level was a large, versatile loft area with three bedrooms and two full bathrooms. The spacious master suite had a walk-in closet, spa like bath featuring a jacuzzi tub, separate glass rain shower, and dual vanities. Palladium windows offered a panoramic view of the community. The bedroom was already furnished with a silver and gray color scheme. The other two bedrooms were spacious as well but empty. Completing the home was a two-car garage with a large deck.

"What do you think of the house?" Martez asked.

"It's beautiful. Do the people who live here plan on moving soon?" I asked.

"The house is in my name, but it's yours. Dad and I are going to pay the mortgage until you are able to. You'll only be responsible for your bills, but you have more than enough in your account to cover that. You don't need to be trying to work while you're pregnant. The bedroom in the basement is mine when I come to visit, and Dad will get the bedroom on the first floor. The extra two bedrooms can be for the kids, or they can share for now, and the other bedroom can be a guest bedroom."

"Thank you so much. I have to call Papa. How did y'all find this and decorate it from Miami?"

"Blaze found it right before you came to Miami. They were in the process of doing construction here, so we were able to make changes and give input. He's been working with the contractors to get everything together for you. We helped design the exterior, kitchen, cabinets, basement, floors, and railings. Lauren helped me pick out the furniture and decorations. Blaze took the time out to be there whenever they needed to deliver something. We kept the other bedrooms empty for when we started getting the baby stuff. I'm staying here for two weeks, and Blaze is going to help me get the twins' room together. By the time I leave, all the rooms will be furnished."

"Thank you, Malakai." I smiled.

Words couldn't explain how happy I was at that moment. Everything I wanted was falling into place, not to mention Malakai was too good to be true. Him taking time out of his busy schedule to do this meant a lot to me.

"You're welcome, McKenzie."

"I'm about to go to Target to get some things for the house and find something to eat. Then, tomorrow, we can go grocery shopping," Martez said.

"Okay, that's fine. You can get something from wherever. I need to go upstairs and lie down for a minute because my back and feet hurt," I replied.

"I'll take her luggage upstairs, then I can go with you," Malakai offered.

"I'm good. Can you stay here with Kenz until I get back?"

"Yeah, I don't have anything planned tonight," Malakai said.

I walked upstairs with Malakai right behind me. When I got to my bedroom, I opened my suitcase and started putting the clothes away that I'd packed. I would get the rest of my things when I told my mom that I was in town. Nobody knew I was back yet, and none of them knew I was pregnant because I had been trying to protect my peace and stay stress free.

I went into the bathroom and took a quick shower. If Malakai wasn't waiting for me, I would've soaked in my Jacuzzi, but I would have plenty of time to do that at a later date. I dried off, put on a sports bra and leggings, then went back into the bedroom where Malakai was lying in my bed with a tank top and a pair of basketball shorts on.

"Where did you get shorts from?" I asked.

"From the small dresser over there with some of my things," he casually said.

I walked over to the small dresser and looked inside the drawers. There were Ethika boxers, tank tops, shirts, shorts, socks, and pants inside.

"Uhm, why do you have a drawer at my house?"

"Because you're my friend, and I'm going to visit you. There might be times that I need to spend the night, and I know you don't like people in your bed with outside clothes. So, unless you want me in your bed naked, I figured I needed clothes."

"I mean, I wouldn't mind you naked in my bed."

"Nah, because if I'm naked in your bed, we're going to be doing more than watching TV, and we both know you're not ready for me yet."

"Blah, blah, blah." I laughed before lying on the bed next to him. I grabbed my phone from the table and sent Tori my address.

"Get up from lying flat on your back. You need to prop up on them pillows if you want to lay on your back."

"I know, but the pillows are soft, and my back hurts."

"Come here, I'll massage it for you."

Malakai sat up against the headboard and opened his legs. I sat between them, and he started giving me a massage. The shit felt good as hell, and I couldn't hold in the moan that escaped my lips.

"That feels so good, Malakai," I groaned.

"Girl, your ass better stop moaning like that."

"I can't help it. That shit feels good as hell."

Malakai continued to massage my back until his phone started ringing. It rang once, and he ignored it until it started ringing again.

"Answer it and tell her I'm busy," he said.

"What? You want me to answer your phone?"

"You heard me. I don't want to talk to her right now, and she'll keep calling until I answer."

I didn't want to answer the phone, but I didn't want him to stop massaging me either.

"Hello," I answered.

"Who the fuck is this? Where is Blaze?" Kim yelled.

"Malakai is busy right now. He said he'll call you later."

"Busy doing what? Bitch, give him his phone. You don't have no business answering it anyway."

I took the phone off my ear for a minute to calm down, but she asked for it.

"Bitch, he's busy making sure I feel good. He'll call you when he's ready to talk to you," I said before hanging up the phone.

Not even a minute after I hung up, Kim called right back.

"You should give me massages more often," I told him.

"I gotcha, ma," Malakai laughed.

I reached over, grabbed his phone, and handed it back to him.

"Kim, what the fuck do you want? She told you I'd call you back," he said.

"Who the fuck is that bitch you with?" I heard Kim scream through the phone.

"Watch your motherfucking mouth. Don't disrespect her by calling her a bitch. You're not my woman, so don't question me. Now, do you want something, or I'm going to hang up?"

"I was trying to see if you're coming over tonight."

"Nah, I already told you I have some shit to take care of."

"So, spending time with another female is more important than coming to see me?"

"I'm about to hang up on your ass. Don't call me back tonight, or I'm going to block you," Malakai stated before hanging up the phone.

"You better be working on getting that bitch out your system because the same way you don't plan on sharing me, I don't plan on sharing you."

"You don't have to worry about that. I don't have a problem with dropping her ass. You just need to worry about meeting up with your baby daddy and getting everything situated with him."

"I'm going to get settled in here first. My appointment is not until next Friday, so I'll contact him a few days before."

Malakai and I started back watching TV until my doorbell went off.

"I'll get that for you," Malakai offered.

Malakai walked down the stairs, then a couple minutes later, Tori walked into my room.

"Heyyy, I missed you so much," Tori beamed.

"I missed you too," I told her.

"Malakai, this is my best friend, Tori. Tori, this is my friend Malakai."

"Nice to meet you, but you can call me Blaze. She's the only one who can call me Malakai, and I'm her future husband. She just doesn't believe it yet," Malakai said.

"It's nice to meet you, Blaze," Tori spoke.

"I'm going downstairs, so y'all can catch up. Martez should be here soon anyway."

"Okay, we'll be down when he gets here," I replied.

"Damn, girl, you said Blaze was fine, but that man is sexy, and his demeanor is on a different level. I'm glad you met him, so he can keep your mind off Chase's dumb ass."

"Girl, I still haven't talked to Chase yet. I'm going to meet up with him soon, though, so I can tell him about the babies and my ultrasound appointment."

"I'm so excited for that. I can't wait to find out what you're having, so I can start planning the baby shower."

"I'm excited too. I'm going to go talk to my mother after my ultrasound and let her know that I'm back up here. I need to get my stuff from the house anyway, and it's best for me to do it while Martez is in town, so him and Malakai can pack for me."

"That makes sense. I love this house, by the way," Tori complimented.

"Thank you, I do too. I have the best father and brother in the world. I have an extra bedroom, so you can come visit whenever you want, especially when the twins get here."

"You already know I'll be here to help you with my God kids."

"I know, that's why you're my BFF." I smiled.

Tori and I had been friends since we were four years old. We went to the same elementary and high school. She was the only girl that I was able to stay cool with outside of my family. We were there for each other through thick and thin. We laughed, cried, and fought together. We both had secrets to take to the grave. She was my personal diary, and I wouldn't change a thing about our friendship.

CHAPTER FIFTEEN
CHASE

The past few months of not talking to or seeing McKenzie had been hell, but I plastered a smile on my face when I was around Diane to try and keep the confusion down. I didn't want to give her a reason to be stressed out. When I first found out Kenzie had up and moved to Miami without us resolving things, I was furious. I was ready to get on the first plane and drag her ass back, but then I thought about Diane and the baby. I thought if I didn't see Kenzie, I'd eventually get over her, but that wasn't true. Truth is, I missed her ass more and more every day.

I checked on her through Aniyah and Tino. She answered Tino's calls as long as he promised not to put me on the phone. During the time Kenzie and I were together, she and my brother had built a friendship. He looked at her like the little sister he never had. At first, I was pissed off that she was answering him while still having me blocked, but I eventually got over it because I was happy that I could at least keep up with how she was doing.

When I made it to the trap house, niggas were playing the game and sitting around while half-naked women were cutting and bagging dope. I spoke to everyone then walked straight to my office to do some work. I was glad Tino had been on his shit, or I'd be way behind after barely being there over the last few weeks.

I sat and counted money for almost an hour before I decided to take a break. After lighting my blunt, I leaned back in my seat, pulled my phone out of my pocket, and scrolled to McKenzie's name. I was about to click on it when Tino walked in.

"What's going on?" Tino spoke as he walked in and sat down.

"Shit, thinking about Kenzie's ass. All I want to do is talk to her and check on her myself, but I know she's not going to talk to me."

"I'm sure she'll come around eventually. She just needs time to figure things out."

"How much time does she need? It's been five months already. What the hell?"

"You lied to her, and she found out through another female. What did you expect to happen? All females aren't as forgiving as Diane."

"I know, but I thought if she loved me, she would have at least given in by now."

"She's weighing all her options. Just give her a little more time."

I sat back in my seat and thought about whether I should tell my brother what's been on my mind.

"You know, I've been thinking. What if Kenzie was pregnant and got an abortion, or she's pregnant and plans to keep my kid from me out of spite, so she's staying in Miami?"

"What would make you think you got her pregnant?"

"We were having sex damn near every day, and I wasn't pulling out. I slept with Diane twice a week and was pulling out, and she got pregnant. I expected Kenzie to be the one to tell me she was pregnant."

"Let me find out you was trying to get Kenzie pregnant."

"I wasn't trying to get her pregnant, but I wasn't doing anything to prevent it either. I didn't care if she got pregnant because she was the person I planned to have a future with," I confessed.

"How's Diane doing? I'm surprised she let you out today."

"She's doing alright, and I've been in the house all week, watching her mope around. I couldn't do it anymore. I'm going home once I finish up here."

Tino and I worked for about forty more minutes before we got up to go. I walked through the house and made sure everyone was cool before leaving. As soon as I made it down the stairs, a car pulled up, and shots were fired. I pulled my gun out and started firing back with Tino right behind me.

"Fuck," I yelled as pain surged through my body.

The car screeched away but not quick enough. Tino and I fired shots through the window and tires, causing it to swerve into a parked car.

We ran over to the car with our guns still out. The guy in the back seat was slumped over dead, and the guy in the passenger seat was close to it. I fired my gun and shot him in the head. The one in the driver's seat was unconscious but had no bullet wounds.

I called K.G. for him and the clean-up crew to get rid of the car and the two dead bodies. Tino tied the unconscious guy up in the basement, so we could question him later and see why they were there.

"Aye, man, you're bleeding. We need to get you to the hospital," Tino said.

"Nah, just take me to the house and let Ma check it out first."

Tino climbed in my car to drive me, and Quan followed in Tino's car. Tino turned the fifteen-minute drive into ten. He called and told somebody I was shot and that we were going to my house, but he didn't tell me who he was talking to.

We got out of the car, and I went straight to the bathroom while Tino went to get our OG. I took my coat and shirt off, then stood in front of the mirror. I was glad to see that I was only shot in the shoulder, but I was nervous with all the blood I was losing.

A couple minutes later, my mother rushed into the bathroom with her medical bag.

"Boy, I told you to be careful out here in these streets," she fussed.

"I was being safe, Ma. I was on my way home when they started shooting at me."

My mother examined me, and there was no exit wound, so she would have to take the bullet out.

"Tino!!!" my mother yelled.

"Yeah, Ma," he answered.

"Put some plastic and a clean white sheet on your brother's bed," my mother told him.

"Ma, you don't have to do that. Just dig it out in here," I said.

"It's not that simple, Chase. There's no exit wound, so it's going to be hard for me to cut you while you're sitting on the edge of a tub. Just take your ass in the room, so I can get that thing out of you because you're losing too much blood."

There was no use arguing with her, so I got up and went to

my bedroom, then lay on the bed. My mother shot something in my arm to numb it, then she used something for the pain. She pulled her scalpel out and started working on my arm. As she finished up my stitches, I heard a voice behind my mother.

"Oh my God. Chase, are you okay?" Kenzie screeched.

I thought I was dreaming because there was no way she was in my bedroom when she was supposed to be in Miami. I shot up in the bed, and pain surged through my body. My eyes immediately fell to her protruding stomach. I was pissed, but I tried my best to keep my composure. I couldn't tell how far along she was, but if she was in my house, then that meant it was a chance the baby was mine.

"Kenzie, what are you doing here? I thought you were in Miami?"

"I've been back here for about a week. Tino called and told me you were shot, so I came here."

"What is that girl doing here?" my mother asked.

"I don't know, Ma, but don't be rude," I replied.

"Hey, Ms. Juliet," Kenzie spoke before sitting in the chair across from my bed.

"Hey, McKenzie," my mother spoke back. I was glad my ma was at least being cordial because I knew she didn't want Kenzie around, but there was nothing she could do about it.

I lay there for about another ten minutes while my mother finished stitching and bandaging my arm.

"You're done?" I asked, eager to get up and talk to Kenzie.

"Yeah, get up, so I can change your sheet because there's blood on it. You should also stay here tonight, so I can check on your arm again."

I got up from the bed and looked over at McKenzie, who was smiling hard as hell while texting on her phone.

"Who the fuck got you smiling so hard?"

"None of your business. We're not together anymore."

"I'm not trying to hear that shit." I snatched her phone and walked to the living room. I had no right to be pissed, but I was after reading her messages with some nigga named Malakai.

"Give me my damn phone back, Chase. I'm not playing with your ass!" McKenzie yelled.

"What the fuck are you supposed to be telling me that he's so concerned about? Could it be that you're pregnant?" I asked, turning to look at her. She looked beautiful, dressed down in a baggy hoodie, leggings, and UGG boots. Her long hair was pulled back in a slick ponytail. She had gained a few pounds since I'd last seen her, but they were in all the right places. Her hips, thighs, and ass were a little bigger now.

"I'm not about to fucking argue with you, Chase. I'll come back tomorrow after you calm down."

"Fuck that. Tell me what the hell is going on," I demanded as I took a step toward her, causing her to take one back.

"Chase, chill. You've been talking about how much you want to talk to her, but now you're going to piss her off, and she's going to leave," Tino said.

I took a deep breath to calm down because Tino was right.

"I'm sorry, Kenzie, come here. I don't want to fight with you."

I walked over and tried to pull her into my arms, but she stepped away again. This time, I grabbed her and pulled her close to me. I tried to hug her, but she stuck her hand out to stop me. My mother walked from the back at the same time, so I let her out first, then joined Kenzie back in the living room.

"Let's sit down and talk," Kenzie suggested.

I sat on the couch, and she sat next to me.

"I just want to apologize again for how everything went down. I never meant to hurt you, and I never should have lied."

"I'm not here to talk about us, Chase. You lied to me, and you have a girlfriend. I'm over that now, and I've come to terms with the fact that we will never be together. I'm seven months pregnant with twins. I found out while I was in Miami that I was already two months pregnant, but I needed to protect my peace and remain stress free. I didn't tell my family here because it would get back to Shavon and your girlfriend. I already fought once while I was pregnant, and I don't intend to do it again."

Well, I'll be damned. I was actually right. I thought I was just tripping with the pregnancy idea. I was glad she didn't get rid of the baby, though.

"Are you back here for good, or are you planning to raise my kids in Miami with some other nigga?" I yelled a little louder than I intended.

"First of all, calm down. I came here so we could have a civil conversation. I'm back up here for good, but whether you're in my kids' lives or not is up to you. I know you have another life outside of me, and I'm not here to disrupt that. If you don't want anything to do with them, I understand. I just felt like you had a right to know."

"Don't insult me like that, McKenzie. I lied to you about Diane, but I was honest about my feelings for you, and I'm always here if you need me. I told you my story, and I would never put my kids through that. Diane lost our baby last month, so there's nothing forcing me to be there now. I can leave her and be with you. We can raise our kids as a family."

"I'm sorry for your loss, Chase, but that's not how this is going to work. You're not leaving that girl and getting with me just because I'm pregnant. Honestly, I can't do the relationship thing right now with anyone. I can only focus on my kids, school, and my mental health."

"Okay, so that means you not fucking no nigga while carrying my kids?"

"Not that it's any of your business, but no. I don't even get down like that."

"Where are you staying? You can move in here when you have the kids, or I can find you your own place."

"Thank you, but no offense, I'm not going to live in a hangout spot with my kids."

"Well, you damn sure can't live where you are now with them. It's barely room for you there, let alone two kids."

"No shit, I'm not stupid. I don't live there anymore. I have my own place in Naperville."

"My bad. I didn't know your father and brother got it for you still."

"Of course, they did. Those are the two men I can count on to never let me down."

"You're right. It's getting late, so why don't you stay here tonight? You can have my bed, and I'll sleep on the couch."

"I don't know if that's a good idea."

"Come on, you don't have anything to worry about. I'll get you a t-shirt to wear."

I walked to my bedroom with Kenzie following me and got a t-shirt from my drawer for her to put on. She pulled the hoodie over her head, and I smiled when I saw her stomach. I couldn't resist reaching over and touching it. She held my hand and moved it over until I felt the babies moving. I had never experienced this with Diane.

I walked out of the bedroom and to the front so Kenzie could change in peace. Tino was sitting on the couch, scrolling through his phone.

"I'm about to go to bed. Can you lock up on the way out?" I asked.

"Congratulations, bro. I'll turn off the lights, and I'll be back tomorrow," Tino said.

"Thank you."

I walked to my bedroom, and McKenzie was already sprawled out in my bed, asleep. Although I told her I would sleep on the couch, I couldn't resist sleeping in the same bed with her, even if it was just for tonight.

I turned the lights off and took off my pants, then climbed in bed and wrapped my arm across her until I fell asleep.

CHAPTER SIXTEEN
MCKENZIE

The following morning, I woke up to Chase's manhood pressing against me. Instinctively, I started rubbing my ass against him. I was horny as hell and in need of an orgasm. When Tino called me yesterday to tell me Chase had been shot, I was in a state of shock. I hopped in my car and came straight over. My intentions were to check on him and go back home. I did not plan to spend the night, and now that his dick was pressed against me, I knew I was about to do something else I didn't plan to do.

"Are you awake?" I asked.

"Yeah. How am I supposed to sleep with you rubbing your ass against me like that? You got my dick rocked up."

"I'm sorry. I know this is wrong to even bring up with you. It's just that I haven't had sex in four months, and these babies have my hormones all over the place. I'm horny as hell and in need of some head and dick."

"You could have told me that last night, and I would have had your lil ass bouncing on my dick then. I've been trying to have self-control and respect your boundaries."

"Well, I'm telling you now, so what you gon' do about it?"

Chase got up, and I turned over on my back. He pulled my shirt over my head and slid my underwear off. Then he grabbed the pillows he was lying on and put them up under me. Hovering over me, he placed soft kisses on my neck, then made his way down to my nipples, sucking on them gently and causing a moan to escape my mouth. My nipples were sensitive, so the sensation of his tongue had me squirming already.

Chase proceeded to trail his kisses lower and lower until he made it to my honeypot.

"Damn, Kenz, you're soaking wet already, baby," he whispered before diving in headfirst. He slowly licked my surface with the tip of his tongue before separating my lips and twirling his tongue on my clit.

"Oh, my God, Chase. That feels so good," I moaned as I closed my eyes tight.

I held onto the back of his head and twirled my hips as I pushed him further into my pussy. His tongue game had me ready to run up the wall.

"Stop fucking moving and cum for me," he ordered as he held my waist down.

Chase went back to his tongue lashing, and it was only a matter of minutes before I came in his mouth. My cream was on his chin as he leaned in and kissed me on my lips. I slid my hand down his boxers and stroked his manhood, causing him to moan.

"Take your boxers off and fuck me," I demanded.

Chase smirked before pulling his boxers off. I winced as he slid the tip inside of me. There was a slight discomfort because it had been a while. I opened my legs so he could put it all the way in. He pushed his hips, thrusting into me harder and filling me completely.

I bit my bottom lip and closed my eyes as Chase hit my spot.

"Shit, Kenz, I missed you so much. You feel so fucking good," he cursed as he slowly rocked his hips.

"Fuck, go faster, Chase," I breathed as I dug my fingers into his back. He immediately fulfilled my request and fucked me faster until I came on his dick.

Chase switched positions with me and propped himself up on the pillows as I climbed on top and slid down his manhood.

"You're so damn beautiful," Chase said as he caressed my cheek.

I held onto his shoulders to keep my balance while I bounced up and down on his dick. I let out a slight moan as I twirled my hips in a circular motion. He used one hand to massage my breast and the other one to squeeze my ass cheek.

"Chaseeee, I'm about to cum, baby," I moaned as I squirted all over his dick.

I got up and turned around, arching my back with my ass in the air.

Chase held onto my waist as he slid inside of me. He grabbed a handful of my hair and stroked me slowly. I gripped the sheets while he pounded in and out of me with precision.

"Cum on this dick one more time," he demanded as he slapped me on the ass.

"Fuck! I'm cumming!" I cried as I threw my ass against him.

"Ugghhh, I'm right behind you." Chase groaned as he buried his seeds inside me.

"Thanks, I needed that," I said as I flopped down on the bed.

"Get your ass up from laying down like that before you hurt my kids."

"Relax, it's a habit. I'm not going to hurt them," I mumbled as I rolled over to my side.

"Get up, so we can shower. We still have some things to discuss, and you need to eat."

I didn't feel like getting up, but Chase was right. We needed to sit down and discuss the kids and my appointments.

Chase and I got out of bed and went to the bathroom. I turned on the hot water in the shower, then brushed my teeth and washed my face. As soon as I stepped foot in the shower, Chase was all over me, ready for round two. After our steamy shower session, I dried off and got dressed back in the clothes I wore to his house since I was going back home once we finished talking.

I headed into Chase's kitchen and looked in the refrigerator. As usual, he didn't have any food, so I didn't know why he mentioned me eating. I walked over to the couch and sat down until Chase came to join me.

"You have no food in your refrigerator," I pouted.

"I know. Tino should be pulling up soon with food."

"I hope it's cooked," I said.

"It is, now let's talk about our kids. When is your next appointment?"

"I have an ultrasound next Friday to find out the sex. They wanted to do it two weeks ago when I was in Miami, but I wanted to wait and talk to you first. I figured you missed the first five appointments, so you should at least be able to go to the rest of them." I shrugged.

"Okay. Make sure to text me the details and your address."

"What you need my address for?"

"Fuck you mean, what I need your address for? I need to know where the hell you and my kids laying y'all head at night."

"Fine, I'll text it to you later, but you're not allowed to pop up without calling first. Just because we had sex today doesn't mean we're getting back to where we were. I need you to respect that and focus on our kids instead of us being together. We're going to co-parent and give them the best life we possibly can. They'll stay with me, and once they're bigger, you can start getting them on your own, granted your girlfriend accepts them."

"That's my house. She has no say in whether my kids can come home with me or not. I'll get her an apartment for herself before I allow her to mistreat them."

"I hear you, Chase. Also, the way you reacted yesterday with my phone, you're not allowed to do that. You don't have to worry about me fucking someone while I'm pregnant, but eventually, after the kids are born, I'm going to move on. You have to respect that in order for us to have a healthy relationship."

"So, I'm supposed to just sit back and allow some other nigga to play daddy to my kids?"

"No matter who I'm with, you're our kids' father, and they will know that, no matter what," I assured him.

Chase was about to respond when Tino came in with bags of food from Ihop.

"Hey, y'all, congratulations on the twins, sis," Tino said.

"Thank you. I hope you're ready for babysitting duties," I told him.

"Of course. I'm going to be the best uncle these kids can have."

I stayed and talked to Tino and Chase until I finished eating, then I went home. When I got there, Martez and Malakai were sitting at the table talking.

After I spoke to them, I went upstairs to my bedroom to change clothes. I put on a t-shirt and a pair of shorts, then climbed in bed and turned on the TV. I was in the middle of watching *Enough* when there was a knock at my door.

"Come in," I called out.

Malakai walked into my room and laid down next to me.

"Do you want to go out to eat tonight, or I can order something?" he asked.

"You don't have to keep coming over here to feed me. Martez already stocked my refrigerator, and I know how to cook."

"I never said you didn't know how to cook. You live on your own, and you're carrying twins."

"Fine. You can order something then. My feet feel like they're starting to swell. Is my brother still downstairs?"

"No, he went to the store to get some paint for the kids' room, so we can start getting it together," Malakai said as he slid to the foot of my bed. He took off my socks and started massaging my feet.

"I told him that he didn't need to do that. I can hire somebody to paint."

"He just wants to make sure you have everything you need before he goes back home because he won't be back until your baby shower."

"Yeah, I know, but he's going overboard."

"Maybe, but that's your big brother. You can't fault him for loving you. How did things go with you and Chase? Do you plan to work on things with him?"

"Things went fine overall once we got past the yelling match. I'm not working on things with him. I told you, I'll never get back in a relationship with him, and I meant that. It would have been different if he cheated, then I could probably have thought about forgiving him, but he had an entire relationship behind my back. We're going to learn how to co-parent. I already told him that he has to be prepared for me to move on."

"I hope he'll listen because I don't want to have to fuck your baby daddy up if he comes over here on some bullshit when I'm here."

"He can't get mad if you're here. He got a girlfriend at home that he lay up with every night."

"That might be true, but I'm sure that didn't stop him from sleeping with you last night. I see the hickey his ass left on your neck."

"I told him it was just sex, and I meant it. It's been five months since I had sex, and you not budging," I said.

"We had this conversation already, McKenzie. You're pregnant, and you're not ready for a relationship yet, so that means you're not ready for me. When I dick you down, you're going to be my woman, and this is going to be the only dick you want and need. I'm not willing to share you with your baby daddy or any other nigga."

"You're having sex with Kim, and y'all not in a relationship," I pointed out.

"That's because I like you and want to be with you. I don't like her like that, and there are no feelings involved from my end. When you're ready, you won't have to worry about Kim anymore. I told you, we gon' do this shit the right way. You've had fucked up relationships, and so have I, which is why we're taking the time to get to know each other as friends first."

"I hear you, Malakai, and I'm not the only one who better be ready because I promise, if you have a baby on me, I'm fucking you and that bitch up."

"You don't have to worry about that. I ain't out here going bareback. The next kid I have gon' be with you when we're married."

I couldn't help but blush at Malakai's words. He was a smooth talker like my father. I could see how my father talked my mother right into his bed because Malakai had me feeling the same way.

Malakai and I continued to talk for almost an hour until I fell asleep on him. I didn't wake up until Martez came and told me the food was there. I went down and had dinner with my brother and Malakai until they had to leave to take care of business. After that, I pulled out my books and started studying.

CHAPTER SEVENTEEN
DIANE

A lot had changed over the past five months between Chase and me. The first couple of days after the mall incident, Chase was coming home every night, but he was barely talking to me, and he slept in one of the other bedrooms. We found out I was four weeks pregnant at my first doctors' appointment. After that, we started sleeping in the same bed and making love again.

Things were progressing well with our relationship, and it felt like the baby was the glue to keep my relationship with Chase together. Last month, I had an ultrasound to find out what I was having. We found out we were having a baby boy, but his heart was no longer beating. It felt like my world came crashing down. What was supposed to be the happiest moment of my life had become a tragedy. It was as if I wasn't meant to be happy. I could still remember that day like it was yesterday.

Chase and I made love that morning, then got dressed. I was slightly cramping, but I didn't think anything of it because that had been happening off and on lately. When I called my doctor, she assured me that it was normal because my baby was growing, so I didn't worry.

During the drive to the hospital, I was a nervous wreck, but Chase tried to assure me that everything was alright. We made it to the hospital and checked in, then went up to ultrasound. After a few minutes, the tech came in to do my ultrasound. She told me I was having a boy, but I needed to wait for my doctor to come and talk to me. I asked what was going on, but she stated she wasn't allowed to tell me, which made me nervous as hell.

About twenty minutes later, my doctor walked into the room with a solemn look on her face. Without even knowing what was wrong, I started crying my ass off. Chase was oblivious to what was going on, but I knew something was wrong with my baby.

My doctor waited for me to calm down before she apologized and told me my baby's heart was no longer beating. She explained that they would do a D&E, which stands for Dilation and Evacuation. It's something that they do to dilate the cervix so they can suction the baby out. The procedure would only take thirty minutes, and they would put me under general anesthesia and give me pain medication.

I had questions, though. I wanted to know how this could happen again. I wanted to know what I did wrong. She claimed it wasn't anything that I did, and my son's umbilical cord was wrapped around his neck.

I was a mess after hearing that, but Chase held my hand until it was time for him to leave the room. He kissed me on the forehead, then walked out. I said a silent prayer for my baby while I waited for them to sedate me. They took about five minutes, then I was injected, and everything went black. When I woke back up, I was in a different room with Chase sitting next to my bed, scrolling through his phone. I was in excruciating pain and ready to go home.

We were at the hospital for another hour before I was discharged. On the way home, we stopped at Walgreens to get my medication. The ride was quiet because Chase and I were both lost in our thoughts. Chase hadn't said anything, and he could barely look at me. I knew he blamed me, and I couldn't be mad at him because this was my fault. I was cramping, and instead of going to the hospital, I ignored the signs. I should have been more safe than sorry.

Chase told me he didn't want a baby, but I got pregnant on purpose anyway. Then, when he finally came around to the idea of us being a family, it was gone in the blink of an eye. I felt that losing the baby was punishment for all the things I did to make Chase stay with me.

When we made it home, Chase helped me out of the car and up to our bedroom. I climbed in bed while he went into the bathroom to shower, and I cried silently until Chase climbed in bed with me.

He whispered in my ear repeatedly that everything was going to be alright as he rubbed his fingers through my hair, only causing me to break down even harder. I don't know how long I lay there crying before I finally fell asleep.

Later that day, I woke up to an empty bed. I looked at the clock and saw that it was already 7:00 pm. I got out of bed and took a shower, then got dressed in a pair of jogging pants and a t-shirt. After that, I walked downstairs and found Chase sitting on the couch watching TV.

He offered to fix me something to eat, but I didn't have an appetite. I couldn't understand how he was sitting there like nothing had happened. I wanted to talk about what happened, but Chase didn't, which pissed me off. He said there was nothing to talk about, and I needed to focus on getting better. I started lashing out, and he took it, but the next day, he suggested I start therapy again. I was against it at first, but then it felt like I was falling into depression, so I went, and the doctor prescribed Prozac for me.

I blamed myself repeatedly, but Chase told me that it wasn't my fault, and it just wasn't the right time for us. My therapist said the same thing, and I was starting to believe it. When the time is right, we'd have kids. If I'm being honest, Chase and I didn't need kids right now anyway. He was heavy in the streets, and I had just gotten hired as a social worker. I didn't bust my ass through college to throw it all away. Chase had been supportive the whole time, so the least I could do was be patient and follow his lead for once.

Chase had been attentive and there for me during this whole process. I was finally feeling like myself again, and all I wanted was for Chase to cuddle with me, but it was eight in the morning, and I had woken up in bed alone for the second time this week. The first time, he claimed he stayed at his mother's house because he got shot. I saw the wound, so I knew that part was true, but I didn't understand why he didn't call me. That made me think he had someone else at his mother's house with him.

Last night, I tossed and turned until almost one in the morning when Chase decided to text and say he wasn't coming home. He said something went down, and he didn't know how long it would take, so he'd be staying at his old house. Part of me wanted to get dressed and drive out there to see if he was telling the truth, but the other part didn't want to know. Instead, I tossed and turned, trying to figure out what could have happened in a week's time to make Chase go back to his old ways. I was starting to think he was cheating on me. I wasn't even sure if he stopped after the McKenzie situation, but if he didn't, he had been covering it up well.

I could be overthinking things, and something could have gone down in the streets last night like he said. It wouldn't be the first time he needed to stay out all night. I knew Chase made his money illegally, but he never went into detail with me about what was actually going on. He didn't allow me to come to any of his traps, and I had never seen him touch drugs. He hadn't given me any indication that he was cheating, and I needed to trust him if I wanted things to work out between us. No one had been calling his phone, and he wasn't having private conversations.

The only person I ever had to worry about Chase leaving me for was McKenzie, and Shavon told me she moved back to Miami after everything happened. I found solace in that. It was sad, but, in a way, I knew that was part of the reason why Chase was still with me.

I lay in bed, staring at the ceiling for almost another hour until I got up and decided to shower because there was no way I was going to fall back asleep. After a quick shower, I dressed in a pair of black jeans and a white t-shirt, then I combed my weave into a ponytail and flopped back on my bed. My follow-up appointment with my doctor was at two, and I hoped Chase would go with me. I picked up my phone and dialed Chase's number, but, of course, he didn't answer. It was still early, though, so that didn't mean he was ignoring me.

I'd give it about an hour to see if he called back before I tried to call again. In the meantime, I would find something to eat and try to relax.

CHAPTER EIGHTEEN

CHASE

The past week had not gone how I expected. I thought after Kenzie and I had sex, things would be back to normal. The only time we talked was if I reached out to her, and even then, the conversation was dry. She didn't want to meet up with me when I asked, and she didn't give me her address. She told me I didn't need it yet and that I'd get it after the baby shower. I knew it was because she didn't want me popping up at her house unannounced, and I had every intention of doing so. I wanted to know what she was up to because I knew it was more to this nigga Malakai than what she told me.

It was 11:00 a.m., and I had just finished showering. I got dressed in a black Gucci jogging suit with a pair of black Timbs. I looked down at my phone and saw that I had four missed calls from Diane. She had been extra clingy lately, and it was getting on my nerves. It was becoming harder for me to fake like everything was good, now that I knew Kenzie was back in town and pregnant with my kids.

It was wrong for me to feel this way, and I did feel bad

about Diane losing our baby. I wasn't a heartless nigga, and I cared about my unborn child. Hell, I still cared about Diane as well. Everything was just so fucked up, and it was nobody's fault but my own. I knew I needed to stop leading Diane on, but at the same time, she was depressed, and I didn't want her to harm herself.

McKenzie's doctor's appointment was at noon, and it was almost twenty-five minutes from my house. I didn't want to be late, so I grabbed my keys and left the house. Once I got in the car, I decided to call Diane and talk to her now because I didn't want her blowing up my phone while I was with McKenzie.

"Why weren't you answering your phone? I've called you four times. You don't know if it was important or not!" Diane yelled into the phone.

"Diane, don't start this shit. I didn't answer the phone because I was asleep. If it was important, you would have called my mom. So, did you want something, or you called me to be on bullshit?"

"I'm sorry. It's just that I missed you and couldn't sleep well without you holding me last night."

"I'm sorry, baby. I texted you and told you some shit went down. I didn't get done until almost three, and I didn't feel like driving out there that late, so I stayed out here," I said, telling half the truth.

The truth was, I took care of business, got there at midnight, and went to bed. I didn't want to be late for Kenzie's doctor's appointment, and I didn't want to answer questions about why I was leaving home so early. Usually, I would go in the house late at night and wouldn't leave back out until after four.

"I know. I just wish you were here. I have a doctor's appointment today at two. Are you able to go with me?"

"I'm not going to make it. Tino just called me about a

meeting for the business we're getting ready to start, and after that, I have to help Ma with something. Aren't you just going for a checkup and to get that birth control in your arm?"

"Yeah, but I still wanted you with me. Afterward, I thought we could go on a date, then go back home and make love. It's been a month, and you've been patient with me. I'm ready for us to get back to normal."

"I'm sorry, baby. I promise I'll make it up to you later tonight when I get home, but I think I should go buy some condoms. I want to at least give that birth control a few weeks to kick in first."

"Okay, I understand, baby. I love you," Diane said.

"I love you too," I replied before hanging up.

I made it to Northwestern Hospital with twenty minutes to spare. After I parked and went inside, I looked at the directory for the ultrasound department, then took the elevator to the third floor. When I got off the elevator, I walked down the hall to the waiting room and saw McKenzie sitting down, scrolling through her phone.

"Hey, you made it on time," McKenzie said, looking up at me.

"Hey, I told you I know how to be responsible, and I'll be at every appointment you have left."

McKenzie was about to respond when her name was called. She got up, and I followed her to the exam room.

"Hey, my name is Asia, and I'll be doing your ultrasound. Are we finding out the baby's gender today?"

"Hey, yes we are," McKenzie answered.

"Alright, I need you to lay back and lift your shirt. I'm going to squirt some gel on your stomach, and it's going to be a little cold.

McKenzie laid back and did as she was told.

"Oh, my, that is cold." Kenzie giggled when Asia squirted the gel on her.

Asia put the transducer on Kenzie's stomach and moved it around.

"These babies are very active. Do they kick you a lot?"

"Yes, especially at night when I'm trying to sleep," Kenzie said.

A 3-D image popped onto the screen as she moved the instrument around. She then clicked a few buttons on her computer to get some images.

"Is everything alright?" I nervously asked. She wasn't saying anything, so I wasn't sure if something was wrong. I had only seen an ultrasound done once, and that was when Diane found out we were having a son, but he had no heartbeat.

"Yes, everything looks good. The babies are positioned right above mommy's bladder. Twin A is a girl, and right next to her is twin B, your baby boy."

"Yessss, that's what I was hoping for," McKenzie beamed as tears fell from her eyes.

I couldn't believe I was getting a son and a daughter. I had the best of both worlds, and I didn't care if I never had any more kids.

"Is there any way that I can hear the heartbeat?" I asked.

"Sure. Give me one minute to print the pictures, then I can get the doppler for you."

I wiped the tears from McKenzie's eyes then placed a kiss on her forehead. Asia rubbed the doppler on Kenzie's stomach, and this time, tears fell from my eyes when I heard the heartbeats.

We finished up at the hospital, then McKenzie followed me back to my house. She had agreed to sit down and have a proper conversation and dinner with my mother. I told her she didn't have to, but she wanted to get it over with.

When we walked into the house, Tino and Quan were sitting on the couch, smoking and playing the game.

"Aww, shit! Kenzie, when did you get back in town?" Quan asked.

"I came back last week," Kenzie replied.

"Does your family know? Your sister didn't tell me you were back, and I was just with her yesterday."

"Yeah, they know. I saw my sister and mother on Wednesday when I went with my brother to get my things from the house. I told them not to tell anyone."

"Why? Are you going back to Miami for good?"

"No, I'm back out here for good, but I have my own place."

Quan was about to ask another question, but I cut him off because I could tell McKenzie was getting irritated.

"Damn, nigga, stop interrogating her," I said.

"I'm going to your room. It's too much smoke out here for me," McKenzie stated before walking away.

"Yo, y'all can stay here and play the game, but y'all gotta stop smoking. She can't be around smoke," I told them.

"My bad, we'll put it out. I didn't know y'all was coming back here," Tino admitted.

I walked back to my bedroom and found McKenzie pulling a shirt over her head.

"You love stealing my clothes."

"Yeah, I hope you don't mind. I need to lay down for a bit."

"Okay, I'll lay with you until you fall asleep."

McKenzie and I lay in bed together, and I rubbed her stomach. She was asleep within ten minutes. After that, I ordered some groceries to be delivered. I needed to start keeping food there because I never knew when Kenzie would come over or if

I would have to stay there. I went back in the front, and the guys were still playing the game.

"If y'all all here, who's at the trap?"

"Tone, Pierre, K.G., and Mike. We're about to get ready and go too. We just stopped here first because K.G. was still doing pick-ups. Are you coming through today?" Tino asked.

"Yeah, I'll be there later this evening. Ma invited Kenzie over for dinner. Once that's done and Kenzie is ready to go, I'll be there."

"Let me take a leak before we go," Quan said.

"So, what is she having?" Tino whispered so Quan couldn't hear.

"It's a boy and a girl," I proudly stated.

"That's what's up, bro. Did she tell you anything about the baby shower yet? I'm ready to get some shit for my niece and nephew."

"It's going to be next month. Tori and her sister-in-law, Lauren, are in charge of it. They'll be sending the details out this week, now that we know the gender."

"Aniyah isn't going to help them? She and Kenzie not close anymore?"

"I don't know much of what's going on with Kenzie right now. I only know what she tells me. I have a lot of questions, but at the same time, I don't ask them because she's still getting used to me being back in her life, and I don't want to push her away again."

"That's understandable. Have you figured out when you're going to tell Diane?"

I sighed at that question because the thought of it gave me a headache. I kept saying I was going to tell her, but then I would back down after I thought of everything that she'd been through.

"I still don't know. I mean, when is the right time to tell

your girl who just lost her baby that the girl you were cheating on her with is back in town and pregnant with twins?"

"Damn, when you put it that way, this is a fucked-up situation."

"Yeah, but it'll have to be soon. I need her to find out from me before she finds out from someone else. Once the twins are here, it's going to be hard to hide it."

"Okay, we'll finish talking when you come by later," Tino said, ending the conversation since Quan was walking back into the room. I trusted Quan, but McKenzie wasn't announcing her pregnancy to everyone yet, so I had to respect that.

Quan and Tino left, so I sat down and played the game for about an hour and a half until the doorbell rang. I jumped up and tried to answer it before it woke Kenzie up. Once I grabbed the groceries, I went in the kitchen to put them away.

"Chase..." Kenzie called out.

"Yeah?"

"Is anybody else here?" she asked.

"No, it's just me and you."

I wondered why she asked that until a couple minutes later, she walked into the kitchen with the t-shirt on and no bottoms. She walked past me and grabbed a bottle of water from the refrigerator and an orange.

"You actually had groceries delivered?"

"Yes. I didn't want to starve you and my babies."

"Well, aren't you nice," she sarcastically stated.

I couldn't keep my eyes off McKenzie's ass while she made her way around my kitchen. The babies were really doing her body good. I didn't have a problem with her shape in the first place, but now her ass was fat as hell.

My dick was hard as hell just from watching her walk. I'd like to blame it on the fact that I hadn't had sex since we fucked last week, but the truth was, she just had that effect on me.

Unable to resist putting my hands on McKenzie, I lifted her and sat her on my table. I slid my hands up her thick thighs until I made it to the brim of her boy shorts.

"What are you doing, Chase? We can't keep sleeping together," Kenzie protested.

"Shhhh, I just need to feel you right now. Look how hard my dick is."

Kenzie's eyes scanned down my body until they made it to my erect dick. She couldn't take her eyes off it, and just like that, I had her where I wanted her. Before she could protest any further, I pulled down her boy shirts and dived in head-first. She was no longer asking me to stop; she was begging me to keep going until she came in my mouth.

I pulled Kenzie off the counter, and she bent over, so I could get the perfect view of her pussy and ass. I dropped my pants and underwear, then carefully slid inside her. She gripped my dick, making it hard for me not to nut prematurely. I pushed myself further in and held onto her waist. Kenzie's shit had always been good and wet, but today, she was like a super soaker.

"Fuck, Chase, I'm about to cum, baby!" Kenzie cried.

I was glad because I didn't know how much longer I could hold out, and I wanted her to at least have another orgasm first.

"Cum for me, ma," I demanded as I picked up the pace a little. I couldn't fuck her the way I wanted to because I was scared of hurting my kids. The last thing I needed was for her to go into labor early.

"It's right there, Chase. Don't stop, pleaseeee, don't stopppp," she moaned as she started squirting on my dick.

"Shit, I'm cumming too," I announced before nutting inside of her.

I helped Kenzie stand up, and she drank some water while she tried to catch her breath.

"I'm going to shower, alone," she said before walking away

Ignoring that statement, I followed her. When I reached the bathroom, I twisted the doorknob, but it was locked. I found it funny that she thought a locked door could keep me out of the bathroom. I walked back to the kitchen, got a knife, then used it to pick the lock. No matter how much she said this was wrong, it felt right to me. If she was going to be around me half-naked, then I was going to hit every chance I got.

I got in the shower with McKenzie, and just as I planned, all it took was for me to touch her in the right places. It was only a matter of time before I had her ass bent over in the shower, screaming my name over and over again. Once we were done, we cleaned each other off, then got out and got dressed.

"I'm serious, Chase. I can't keep sleeping with you. You need to be working on your relationship with Diane or leaving her alone," McKenzie said as she flopped on the couch.

"If I leave her, are you going to give us another shot?"

"No, that's not how this is going to work. We need to work on rebuilding our friendship and co-parenting. I have to be able to trust you again, and right now, I can't."

"Okay, I don't like that idea, but I understand. We can be friends with benefits." I smirked.

McKenzie rolled her eyes at me and turned the TV on. I couldn't help but laugh at her. We watched *Bad Boys II* then talked a little longer until my mother called and said dinner was ready.

CHAPTER NINETEEN
MCKENZIE

Chase and I sat on his mother's couch while she worked in the kitchen. I needed her to hurry up because I had no plans to stay out there tonight, and Martez would have a fit if I drove home late. He already didn't like me driving alone. He said it wasn't safe with me this far in my pregnancy because my back and feet ached so much. I understood where he was coming from, and I didn't really leave my house unless I was with him, Malakai, or Tori. I didn't know what I would do when Martez went back home. He'd been spoiling me like crazy. I was thinking about having Tori move in with me temporarily until after I had the twins. My biggest fear was going into labor while alone at home with no one to help me get to the hospital.

Malakai lived about fifteen minutes from me, and he always said he was only a call away, but he was also a busy man. He not only had legit businesses, but he had illegal businesses that he had to take care of as well. I didn't want to become dependent on him, and the last thing I wanted was to seem needy. I refused to allow a man to make me feel like I needed him. Malakai was my friend, so I took the initiative to call and text him because I wanted to show him that I was interested, but I didn't call him to do things for me.

Everything Malakai did for me was because he wanted to do it on his own. I didn't have a problem asking a man for things if I was with him, but Malakai and I were not together. I was afraid I'd run him away before we even got our shit together. Trusting him was something else that scared me. I went the friendship route with Chase and got to know him first, and in the end, I found out that I didn't know him as well as I thought I did. I'd like to believe Malakai wouldn't do me like that because I could just feel it in my soul that he was different, but I didn't know.

I had to be mindful and really think about my decisions from now on. Anything I did would not only affect me, but it would affect my kids as well. Malakai claimed that he was willing to be there for the kids and me, so I guess only time would tell how serious he was.

"What is taking your mother so long? I could have made me something to eat in all this time it's taking her," I complained.

"I don't know. Let me go check." Chase got up from the couch just as my phone started ringing. I looked down at the phone and saw that it was Malakai.

"Heyyyy," I sang into the phone.

"Hey, beautiful, when will you be home?"

I looked down at my phone and saw that it was already 4:30 pm.

"Hopefully, I'll be there by seven. I'm about to have dinner with Chase's mother now. You coming to see me or something?"

"Yeah, I have some business I'm about to take care of right now, then I have to pick my kids up. Martez called and told me the stuff for the nursery was delivered, so I'm going to help him put it all together. I just wanted to check on you and see what you're having since your brother wouldn't tell me."

"I told him that I was going to tell you myself. It's a boy and a girl, though."

"Congratulations, you were right."

"Thank you, I have to go. I'll see you later when you come by."

"Alright, see you," Malakai stated before hanging up the phone.

I put my phone in my pocket as Chase and his mother set plates of food on the dining room table.

"Sorry it took me so long. I was waiting on the rolls to finish," Juliet said.

"It's fine," I replied as I got up from the couch.

I walked over to the table and sat down. There was baked chicken, rice pilaf, green beans, and dinner rolls. The food looked good, and I was ready to dig in. We all made our plates before Juliet started talking.

"Chase told me you had a doctor's appointment today. What are you having?"

"A boy and a girl." I smiled.

I almost went crazy when I found out I was having twins. I had no idea what the hell I was going to do with one kid, let alone two. Now I can't wait to meet my bundles of joy. I already loved them more than anything, and they weren't even here yet.

"Okay, how far along are you?"

"I'm seven months."

"How sure are you that those are my son's kids? Are you willing to get a DNA test?"

"Excuse me? I'm not getting a DNA test done. I know who I was sleeping with." Chase's mother had caught me off guard with her question. I couldn't believe she was insinuating that I was a hoe or something.

"Ma, chill, I don't need a DNA test done. She got pregnant while we were together."

"No, Chase, I'm just trying to be practical about this situation. She disappears for months, and then, all of a sudden, she comes back, telling you that she's pregnant and it's yours? If she knew she was pregnant by you, why didn't she reach out when she first found out?"

"You don't have to ask him questions about me like I'm not sitting here. I knew he was my kids' father from the beginning, but I wanted a stress-free pregnancy for as long as I could have one."

"Well, you should have thought about that before you got pregnant by a man with a girlfriend. What did you expect to accomplish by keeping these kids? What do you want from my son? You need money or a house? Tell me, what is it? I know it can't be a relationship because he's already in one, and she's my future daughter-in-law. I will never see you as that. I could never respect someone like you."

"Ma, that's enough. You are out of line!" Chase yelled.

"No, let her finish. Let her get it all out of her system now because I guarantee you this is the first and last time she will ever get to disrespect me in my face," I fumed.

"What is that supposed to mean?" Juliet challenged.

"It means exactly what I said. I respect my elders, and out of respect for you being Chase's mother, I'm going to say this in the nicest way possible. I'm not sure how much you know or what you know about me, but I don't need Chase, and I damn sure don't need you in me or my kids' lives. I don't need a house from Chase because I already have one, and even if I didn't have one here, I have a place in Miami to live. I'm not some hood booger that's out here broke with no guidance or parents. I am well-loved by both my parents and the rest of my family. I only came back and told Chase about my kids as a courtesy. I told him that he didn't have to be in my kids' lives because they'll be good regardless. Let's be real. Look at me. I can guarantee you that it won't be hard for me to get my kids a stepdaddy."

"Wait, what the fuck do you mean you can find my kids a stepdad? I'm the only daddy they will ever have. I'll knock you and that nigga's wig back," Chase interrupted to threaten me.

I ignored him and put my hands up to stop him from talking while I continued my rant with his mother.

"You ask why I chose to continue this pregnancy, even though I knew Chase had a girlfriend? Him having a girlfriend doesn't have shit to do with me or my kids. I don't want Chase anymore, but let's be clear, if I wanted him, your future daughter-in-law would be a distant memory. Just know he's only still with her because I don't want him. I already told him that I'll never start a relationship with him again, so I don't ever plan on being your daughter-in-law anyway.

"I didn't fall for and get pregnant by another woman's man. I fell in love and got pregnant by my man. The man I thought I would have a future with. It's not my fault that you raised a lying cheater. You were around me and in my face, knowing he had a girlfriend, and not one time did you say anything to me about it. Instead, you plastered a fake smile on your face. Where was this loyalty for your future daughter-in-law then? That says more about you than it does about me," I snapped.

"Listen, little girl, I don't know who you think you're talking to—" Juliet started, but I cut her off.

"No, you listen. As far as I'm concerned, we don't have anything else to talk about. I came to have a civilized conversation about my plans with the twins. I didn't have to sit down and talk to you about anything. Chase is the only one who needs to know what's going on with me. You don't have to like me, but you will respect me if you want to be in your grand-kids' lives."

"You can't stop me from seeing them if they're my son's kids."

"Call my bluff and disrespect me again. At the end of the day, I am their mother, and I will have the last say in who they can and can't be around."

"Okay, just answer this, then. Do you plan on letting my son get his kids on his own? What is he supposed to tell his girlfriend about them? If he stops sleeping with you, are you going to try to keep the kids away from him?"

I couldn't help but chuckle at the audacity of her line of questioning. As if it was my responsibility to shield his girl-friend and her feelings.

"What he tells his girlfriend is not my concern. It's not my job to care about her feelings. Chase is the one committed to her. When my kids are a bit older, yes, they can go with Chase, but until then, no, they will not be going with him. He can come to my house to see them, or I can bring them out here to let him spend time with them. As far as me sleeping with him, that's none of your business. I would never stop him from seeing them unless he's a danger to their wellbeing."

"Ma, if I knew you were going to act like this, I never would have told McKenzie to come to dinner with you. Half the ques-tions you're asking her, you already know the answers to because I told you. You can't fault her for what's going on. I'm the one you should be mad at. I'm the one who fucked up, but I can't tell you what you want to hear or what Diane will want to hear. When I got with McKenzie, I went about things wrong, but I won't call her or my kids a mistake. I will be there for my kids regardless of what you or Diane says. If she can't forgive me, then so be it. I'll be moving back out here and making some changes in my life."

"I'm sorry, but I hold both of you accountable for what's going on. Diane just lost your second child last month, and now you're about to throw it in her face that you got two kids on the way by somebody else? That will break her, Chase. You need to just keep this to yourself, at least until the kids are a little older, and you'll have them on your own. Until then, you should be able to get away with hiding it. You were able to sneak around all that time at first with no problem."

"Alright, I've heard enough. This conversation no longer concerns me, so I'll be leaving."

"But you haven't even touched your food," Juliet said.

"I lost my appetite, so I'll find something later. I meant what I said, though. It's on you whether you'll be in your grandkids' lives or not," I reiterated before getting up.

I walked over to the living room, put my coat on, and grabbed my keys and purse. Chase was heavy on my heels, trying to stop me, but there wasn't shit he could say to make me stay in his mother's house another minute. Juliet was lucky she was Chase's mother, or I'd have cursed her baldheaded, no edge, Jenny off the block ass out. She was too damn old to be so God damn messy and in her grown son's business.

I opened the front door, but before I could walk all the way out, Chase gently grabbed me by the arm and pulled me back into the house.

"Please, I need you to calm down before you leave. I don't want you driving home angry and wrap yourself around a pole. I'm sorry for my mother's behavior, and I will talk to her. I promise, the next time you see her, she won't be like that."

"I don't need you to apologize for her, but you do need to talk to her because you know I don't tolerate disrespect. The next time, I won't be so nice, and I'll put her all the way in her place."

"Okay, don't stress about this. I promise I'll fix everything, and my mother will come around. Now, drive safe, and call me when you get home," Chase said. He pulled me into his arms and planted a kiss on my forehead.

"What the fuck is going on here?" a female voice screeched.

I turned around and was face to face with Diane. Chase and I were so busy going back and forth that we never even noticed her walk in the house. This was just my luck; I should have followed my first mind and gone home after my doctor's appointment instead of agreeing to this dumb ass dinner.

I looked up at Chase, and his eyes were big as saucers. He looked like a dear caught in headlights. If I wasn't so pissed, I might actually have found humor in this shit. I had enough drama for one day, though. I was hungry, and my feet hurt, so I walked out the door and left Chase to deal with that shit.

To Be Continued...

ALSO BY KEVINA HOPKINS